I0729170

# AIDEN

## The Mavericks, Book 18

# Dale Mayer

AIDEN: THE MAVERICKS, BOOK 18
Beverly Dale Mayer
Valley Publishing Ltd.

Copyright © 2022

All rights reserved. Except for use in any review, the reproduction or utilization of this work in whole or in part by any electronic, mechanical or other means, now known or hereafter invented, including xerography, photocopying and recording, or in any information storage or retrieval system, is forbidden without the written permission of the publisher.

This is a work of fiction. Names, characters, places, brands, media, and incidents are either the product of the author's imagination or are used fictitiously. Any resemblance to actual events, locales, or persons, living or dead, is entirely coincidental.

ISBN-13: 978-1-773365-42-8
Print Edition

# Books in This Series:

Kerrick, Book 1

Griffin, Book 2

Jax, Book 3

Beau, Book 4

Asher, Book 5

Ryker, Book 6

Miles, Book 7

Nico, Book 8

Keane, Book 9

Lennox, Book 10

Gavin, Book 11

Shane, Book 12

Diesel, Book 13

Jerricho, Book 14

Killian, Book 15

Hatch, Book 16

Corbin, Book 17

Aiden, Book 18

Boxed Sets and Bundles
https://geni.us/Bundlepage

# About This Book

What happens when the very men—trained to make the hard decisions—come up against the rules and regulations that hold them back from doing what needs to be done? They either stay and work within the constraints given to them or they walk away. Only now, for a select few, they have another option:

The Mavericks. A covert black ops team that steps up and break all the rules … but gets the job done.

Welcome to a new military romance series by *USA Today* best-selling author Dale Mayer. A series where you meet new friends and just might get to meet old ones too in this raw and compelling look at the men who keep us safe every day from the darkness where they operate—and live—in the shadows … until someone special helps them step into the light.

Aiden has high hopes for his own mission, but Las Vegas and a woman accused of killing her own husband wasn't it. Then he finds out it's a special request from a man he's long respected and that the woman in question was his cousin. Even more confusing is the series of other murders that, according to the local law enforcement, are linked to her as well.

Toby's life has been one long nightmare, and, just when a light shines in to save her, and she hopes she will survive this after all, the cops decide she's the one who murdered her husband. Hardly … but, if she'd had the guts and the lack of concern for spending the rest of her life in jail for getting justice, then she'd have done it.

But, as it was, if they can't figure out who and what is going on, she'll be spending her life in prison regardless. And that would be a shame, considering she'd just met Aiden, one of the most interesting men to cross her path. Now if only he'd been here years ago, before her world went off the rails …

**Sign up to be notified of all Dale's releases here!**
https://geni.us/DaleNews

# PROLOGUE

A IDEN BRONTE WALKED into his bedroom and stretched. The last few days had been calm, relaxing, and he'd even spent some time with family. Hearing the phone ring, he looked to see who it was. "Hey, Mom."

"How are you doing? Wanted to tell you that your dad and I decided to take a cruise next month."

"Good," he said, and then he frowned. "Isn't that like short notice?"

"I think that's why your father wants to do it. There was an incredible deal, and he wants to go."

"Sounds good. Besides, I don't know where I'll be next month anyway."

"Ah, so that means you can't come with us then."

"Well, I don't know that I can or I can't, but I would say it's probably a no."

"Right."

But she didn't appear to be concerned; in fact, she appeared to be more than excited.

"If there's a chance to see you over the next couple days, it would be nice."

"I'm kinda on call, Mom. We'll see." Their call was over soon, and he got up and had a quick shower. When he came out, he'd missed a call. He immediately dialed, and, when Corbin answered the phone, Aiden asked, "Hey, you guys surviving?"

"More than surviving." Corbin yawned. "Playing house is great. You should try it."

"Even though she's got a baby coming?"

"Absolutely. You know me. I never really figured I would have a family at all. So this is just fine."

"Good. So why the call? What's going on?"

"What's going on is you're shipping out."

"I am?"

"You are. You ready?"

"Hell, yes. Do I get anybody partnered with me?"

"Well, you do, but, in this case, I'm not so sure how that'll work. Do you remember Mountain? Mountain Bear Rode?"

Mountain was one of those huge monster-size guys. "Of course. Who doesn't?"

"He's supposed to be coming on board with the Mavericks too."

"Really? I thought the Mavericks were getting their budget slashed. Also I thought Mountain was heading back up north. Canada or someplace?"

"I think something's afoot with the Mavericks. I'm not exactly sure what's going on."

"Interesting," Aiden said, with a quick frown. "That's fine, as long as I fulfill my obligation, then I'm free and clear, right?"

"You are, indeed. And believe me. I've got Nellie here trying to get me out of it too."

"Yeah, especially now that you've got a family on the way," he said in a teasing note.

"You're absolutely right, but Mountain has a different issue altogether, and he needs us. I'm not sure what that deal is, but he's coming on board to help you first, and you'll be helping him out too. I just don't have all the details."

"Where am I going?" He quickly dressed, while he was talking on the phone.

"You're leaving in twenty minutes. Mountain will be there, with wheels."

"And where are we going?"

"Vegas."

"Vegas? What's in Vegas?" He was stunned at that location. He'd only been stateside for a few days as it was.

"A series of loan sharks involved in gambling and supposedly an innocent victim in it all."

"Yeah, in Vegas is there such a thing?"

"It looks like somebody is laundering money."

"Hardly our deal either." He frowned. "This sounds bizarre for us."

"Just like my mission, sometimes strange things happen."

"Fine. What's going on?"

"The innocent victim is our card dealer, Toby. She's been charged with murder, released on bail. I am told that she's at home in isolation."

"And we care, why?"

"Well, for one, this is not so much a paid job as it's something to do with Mountain. Hopefully he'll tell you more when he picks you up."

"Is it personal?"

"Very, but also something else." Corbin sounded frustrated, which was unusual and unnerving.

"Okay," Aiden said slowly, "that's just confusing."

"I know. Sorry. I'm not trying to be cryptic, but I'm just not getting very much in the way of intel either."

"Hey, that's not how we're supposed to work."

"I know. Believe me. Yet it has to do with Mountain."

"Fine. So I'm supposed to go to Vegas and to help solve a crime and to free somebody who is supposedly up for attempted murder charges?"

"No, not just attempted murder but first-degree murder."

"Who did she supposedly kill?"

"Her husband."

"Well, shit, that alone makes her a good suspect."

"I know, right? Everybody loves to take out their ex. But, according to her, she had nothing to do with it."

"You could have sent me anywhere in the world, and you send me to Vegas? You are going soft."

"I know. Sorry, bro. Not only that but it's not an op that we normally deal with. But, hey, lots of the cases lately have been pretty off the wall."

"If you say so," he snapped. "This is just a BS case."

"Maybe, but it's Mountain's case."

"But it's not supposed to be a Mountain case."

"I know. That's what's weird about it. Anyway he's picking you up in a few minutes. See if you can get more info out of him."

"Yeah, you can bet I will. And thanks."

"Once we're done with this case, I'd like to see you settle close to us."

"Why would you want that?"

"So you can start a family, and so we can stay friends."

"*Ha, ha.* Nobody is in my life. You know that."

"True. But I also know nobody was in my life when I did my last op too."

"No way. Somebody charged with murder doesn't sound

like my kind of partner."

"Well, that's one of many."

"What do you mean, *one of many?*"

"I think they're looking to pin four murders on her."

"Jesus Christ. Why?"

"Because they're all guys she's dealt cards for. They were at her table, winning big. Yet, when they were found dead, no winnings were on them."

"So where's the money then?"

"Believe me. That's something that everyone would like to know. So add it to your list. Find out where the money went."

"Great," he muttered. "I'm out."

And, with that, he grabbed his travel bag he'd had ready since he got back to his place and locked the front door. He walked down to the curb. He hadn't even dropped his bag, when Mountain drove up in a military jeep. Aiden took one look, smiled, threw his bag in the back, and laughed. "The only reason you got a jeep is because you can have the roof off and not hit your head."

Mountain looked at him, and something in his icy gaze warmed slightly. He gave a clipped nod and said, "Nice to see your sense of humor is still there."

"Well, mine is. Where's yours?"

"Frozen," he snapped, "but I'll give you the details on the drive."

"You better," he said, settling into the passenger seat, "because I'm a little confused what kind of a deal this is."

"In a way you got the lucky job, as you might not even have to assist on the next one," he said, "because I've got something going on in the background that's big. It's deep. It's dark, and I need big-time help. Only no one believes we've got a problem, … yet."

"Good enough," Aiden said. "You know me. I'm always there for the rescue."

# CHAPTER 1

**A**IDEN RODE IN the jeep to the airport, where Mountain put his vehicle into long-term parking. As they walked up to the boarding area with their bags over their shoulders, Aiden asked in a low tone, "When will you tell me what this is all about?"

Mountain gave him a hard look. "You know as much as I do."

He snorted at that. "Like hell. Apparently you have some connection, so that this is your case." Aiden hated the fact that the tone of his voice noted this case was supposed to be his.

At that, Mountain shook his head. "No, it's not my case. It's your case. I am, however, connected to the case."

"In what way?"

"Toby is my cousin," he stated.

Aiden came to a dead stop and looked at him. "Seriously?"

"Yeah." Mountain kept walking; Aiden quickly caught up. "I told my father that I would check into it, but he and his brother weren't happy about that. To them she's ruining their name. But they also don't want me involved. They'd rather cut her loose to drown. That's not my style."

"I gather you don't get along?"

"Not enough. Not in a while. And our fathers haven't

gotten along in a long time. I'm not sure they even know what I do."

"And what about Toby?"

"We used to be close," Mountain admitted. "I don't even know why she's still up in Vegas or what kind of trouble she's in. She's a math genius, which has gotten her in trouble before."

"Well, that would be a good reason to end up in Vegas," Aiden noted, "as long as she's not card counting. … I still don't understand what this has to do with anything else."

Mountain didn't say anything for a long moment. They caught their flight at the last minute, entering the plane before the door closed behind them. Finding their seats, they sat down, thankful that it was a short flight.

Aiden looked over at Mountain. "You've got some other gig going on?"

"Let's just say that I've tapped into something that could be pretty big and pretty ugly."

"Tell me more." Aiden turned in his seat to face his buddy. "Is this known by anybody else?"

"Nope. I'm pretty sure whatever I say will just blow the lid off something, an international joint operation, but I have to get some support for a mission to confirm. It's bigger than me."

"And you don't want to go to your boss?"

"Well, right now," Mountain replied, his lips twitching, "I don't really have one."

"What about the Mavericks?"

"Potentially the Mavericks will have my back on this, but I can't be sure. It's one of the reasons I'm doing this job."

"You know, Corbin told me something about it, but he

didn't really give me any details."

"No. Not a whole lot of details to give." At that, Mountain settled into his seat and closed his eyes. "I'm catching five."

If there was ever an immediate shutdown, that was it. Aiden leaned back, ready for this flight to be over with. Pulling up his cell phone, he quickly sent Corbin a message, confirming they were on the flight. He got a thumbs-up as a reply. He smiled at that, wondering just what his own life would look like after this op. It's the kind of work he'd been doing for a very long time. However, watching Corbin and his new partner and her very burgeoning belly—who thankfully survived her ordeal in great shape—Aiden had started to wonder about his own future.

He'd often thought that there wouldn't be one. He'd always gone on missions with the idea, if he were the one who didn't make it back, it would be okay because he was the one who didn't have anybody waiting for him. Now, all of a sudden, he kept thinking it would be a hell of a nice thing if he *did* have somebody waiting for him—something else Corbin had changed for Aiden. And yet that wasn't necessarily a good thing, particularly when nobody was in his orbit.

He looked over at Mountain, who was starting to stir. Aiden waited until his buddy appeared to be cognizant, but then he hopped up and went to the washroom at the back of the plane. When he returned, Aiden said, "So, tell me more about your cousin."

"She's smart, too damn smart."

At that, Aiden frowned. "Is there such a thing?"

"Yeah, there is," Mountain confirmed. "She should have been off in university, but her parents wouldn't pay for her to go. And then, by the time she was old enough and mature enough to tell them to flip off, she no longer knew what she wanted to do. She keeps trying to get rid of her no-good on-and-off-again boyfriend from high school, where that whole scenario sucked from day one. She hooked up with him a couple years ago, where he promptly dumped her and took off with her best friend."

"Nice guy," Aiden quipped, "but a story I'd heard many times before, same song, different singers."

"I know," he agreed. "Then the bad penny turned up again, and, thing is, they got married, and I don't know why."

"Oh, ouch."

"Yeah. That's where she got pretty stupid."

"You just said she was too smart for her own good."

"I asked her why the hell she was marrying the loser guy, and she told me that she didn't have any choice."

"What does that mean?"

"I'm not sure. And they only got married a couple weeks ago, and now he's dead."

"Okay. So hang on. She married the louse two weeks ago, and now he's dead, and she's charged with his murder?"

Mountain nodded. "Right. It all happened so fast that I'm not even sure what the details are, and she hasn't been talking to me at all."

"And yet you mentioned you were close."

"Close as kids and yet not close enough lately apparently." He growled. "I also told her that I could solve this, and she just gave me a flat stare and told me not to bother."

"Meaning that she feels guilty and deserves whatever is coming her way?"

"Well, I hadn't considered it in quite that way," Mountain replied, "but I guess that's always one option."

"Do you really believe she didn't kill him?"

"She says she didn't, and I believe her."

"Okay. Then she feels trapped by something."

"Toby should never have married him, so I'm not exactly sure what the deal is there."

"Right. I'll ask this," Aiden began, "and you won't like it."

At that, Mountain's jaw twitched. "What else is new?"

"Is there a child involved?"

He looked at him. "That's not exactly what I thought you would ask."

"No, but a lot of women would do a lot of things to protect a child."

"Blackmailed into marrying this guy to protect a child? That doesn't make much sense."

"None of this makes any sense," Aiden agreed, "but it will. You know that we just have to get all the answers, and she apparently isn't helping out."

"As far as I know, there's no child," Mountain replied.

Aiden continued with his questions. "Could it be that you just don't know about it yet? Is it likely to be, and none of her family would know about it? Have they not visited her in a long time?"

"No. No one is close. Emotionally, that is. Her parents live in Vegas, but they are worthless. When Toby last got rid of this bad boy, she told me that she had known better than to go back to him and that she wouldn't do it again. She was making plans for a future. Vegas was not it, but it was a means to the end to get the money to go to college. She wanted to be a scientist."

"How old is she?"

"Twenty-eight," Mountain replied. "And she knew that was a late start for college, but she refused to believe that it was too late."

"Of course not. So you feel she was pressured into marrying him."

"Yes. At least, I want to believe that," he added, "because I don't want to believe she went back of her own volition."

"Which you know happens more often than not."

"Yeah, I get that, but that wasn't normal for her."

Aiden paused. "So what was the reason for going back-and-forth?"

"She did tell me that his sister had something to do with her going back to him the last time or the time before that."

"What did the guy's sister have to do with it?"

"She has a mental disability, and the boyfriend was responsible for her."

Aiden frowned. "This bad boy never outgrew his responsibility for somebody who is mentally challenged?" There was no hiding his surprise.

Mountain shrugged. "Apparently he loves his sister."

"And why would that have anything to do with Toby staying with him?"

"I'm not sure. I do know that she really loved the sister too."

"That's a hell of a reason for staying in some crazy guy's orbit unless …" He stopped, looked over at Mountain. "With the sister having mental limitations, that brings in the 'child' feature I mentioned earlier, doesn't it? Is Toby the kind to protect?"

"Absolutely." Mountain nodded. "And then something happened, and I'm not sure what."

"Okay. According to Corbin, the cops are looking at

charging Toby with four other potential murder charges."

"And I don't get that at all." Mountain stared ahead. The seat belt light came on, and he added, "We're getting out of here soon."

"I still need more of the story."

"You'll get it, but from her."

"Will she talk to you?"

"That's the hope," he muttered. "However, at this point in time, I'm not sure I know her at all."

"And yet you promised you could help fix it."

"Yeah. And the two fathers wouldn't take me up on my offer to help her."

"So, lots of family issues are involved."

"Yep."

"What about your parents?"

"What about them?" Mountain replied. "I have nothing to do with them either. My birth mother died giving life to me. My so-called dad remarried soon afterward, getting a housekeeper and cook and babysitter in the bargain. She hated me. I always reminded her of Dad's first wife."

Aiden stared at Mountain, surprised.

His buddy shrugged. "The family is messed up, and I mean all of the family."

"So, Toby's family too?"

"I would have thought she was the straightest of them all, … but now I'm not so sure."

Aiden nodded. "Let's go take a look around Vegas and see what we can find."

As soon as they landed and walked outside, they headed over to the rental vehicles and picked up an SUV. Mountain looked at it and shook his head. "Couldn't we get something with no top on it?"

"Like what?" Aiden asked.

"A jeep."

"You know that won't be easy. And they didn't have any cheap jeeps available."

"*Great.*"

Aiden watched as Mountain folded his huge frame into the passenger side. With his knees close to his chest, he shook his head and popped the seat as far back as possible, just so he could get his knees down.

"Shit!" he muttered.

"I can see why you don't like to travel commercial for the same reason."

"You saw the lack of leg room on the plane," Mountain noted. "You saw me not move."

"Right. I guess military transport is a lot easier."

"And we should have done that," he replied.

"You're right. We will next time."

"I booked it," Mountain said. "Serves me right."

Aiden didn't say anything to that. "I'm hearing an awful lot of guilt in your voice."

"I don't even know if it's guilt," Mountain admitted. "Toby was the sweetest kid though. And I do feel like something blew up in her world."

"Of course you do," Aiden agreed, "but that doesn't mean you could have stopped it."

At that, Mountain shook his head and shrugged. "Doesn't mean I was there to help her out either."

Aiden wondered what to do with that. Of course it was the truth. It was hard to look at things that went wrong around you and to see that maybe you could have done something to help but didn't. Too often everybody just kept busy in their own lives. Meanwhile things blew up, before you even had a chance to realize that something needed to be done.

Aiden followed Mountain's directions until they got to the address they were looking for. Standing outside of the vehicle, Aiden looked up at the small home and asked, "Is it hers?"

"It's one of her father's rental properties," Mountain explained.

"What does her father do?"

"He runs a casino. You'll find almost everybody here is involved in the industry one way or another."

"Is that how she got her job?"

"No." Mountain shook his head. "She wouldn't take a job from him." And, with that, Mountain frowned and looked over at Aiden. "Come on. Let's go hear the story from her firsthand."

When Toby opened her front door, she stared at Aiden in confusion. Then her gaze landed on Mountain. Her face lit up, but then, almost as if it took a force of will, she wiped it clean and gave him a blank look. "Wow. What the hell brought you back?"

Mountain glared at her. "You knew I would come—as soon as you let me know you were in trouble."

"Well, I didn't let you know that I was in trouble, now did I?" she asked in an odd tone, as she walked back into her living room. "You might as well come in though, knowing you won't leave anytime soon."

At that, Aiden looked over at Mountain, who just shrugged. "She's right. I'm not. We have a lot of shit to sort out first."

Aiden stepped inside, not particularly liking the innuendos floating around him. As he walked in, he looked around the small living room, noting not a whole lot of furniture was here, as if she didn't have a whole lot of money. He wondered if the cops had looked at any of that, considering how, if she had stolen money from any of these dead gamblers, she sure as hell wasn't spending any of it. But then that wasn't necessarily an issue because a lot of people waited until they moved and spent it then.

As he sat down in the living room, he looked over at her. "You obviously know Mountain. I'm Aiden."

She looked at him and frowned. "I may have heard that name in the past."

He shrugged. "Mountain and I've known each other for a long time."

She nodded, cast a sideways glance at her cousin, and snapped, "At least he's good at keeping up with some people."

Aiden looked from Mountain to Toby and added, "Look. I don't know what's going on between the two of you, but I would like to be clear. Get past it, so it doesn't interfere in our work."

"Too late," she stated immediately. "I'm Toby by the way."

He nodded. "And I am here to help. Mountain is too."

She shook her head, gazing at the two men. "This isn't your doing."

"I told you that you should've just asked for my help," Mountain said.

"That wouldn't do me any good, would it? And I sure as hell don't want the families involved."

"Why don't you want them involved?" Aiden asked.

She frowned at both men again, then addressed Aiden. "Has Mountain not given you the full details?"

At that, Aiden shook his head. "He's been remarkably tight-lipped about it all, and it would be really nice to know what the hell is going on."

The two relatives shared a look, and then her shoulders slumped. "I don't even know what you're here for," she replied. "It's not as if this is anything you can help with."

TOBY STARED AT the two men. Her cousin just made her heart ache, bringing up so many hard feelings in so many ways. Yet she couldn't remember what was the core of it. All of it paled now, given everything that had torn apart her world since then. Except that she was different, and so was he. She sagged into a chair and stared at the newcomer, Aiden. "I get that you're probably one of those hero kind of guys who's here to help rescue the damsel in distress," she stated, "but sometimes no rescue can happen."

"And sometimes you just need a little faith," he argued calmly. "I have no intention of failing, regardless of what you may think."

She stared at him for a moment. "I don't even know what I think anymore," she admitted softly. "And, if you think you can do anything to help, that would be lovely."

"I need to know a few things," Aiden began. "One, is anything between you and your cousin here that will stop you from helping us or will interfere in our work?"

She smiled. "The only thing between Mountain here and me that's a problem," she replied, "is the fact that he told me to walk away from my ex-boyfriend. So, when things changed, and I went back to my ex, I felt like I needed to stay away from Mountain. When you let people know your feelings in a rather strong manner, it's a little hard to go back to them and ask for help."

"No, it isn't," Mountain countered. "You just move on from the bastard."

She nodded. "I didn't kill him, you know?"

"I know you didn't," he agreed, looking at her. "I never thought you did."

"You're the only one who didn't then."

"What I don't know is why you married him," Mountain admitted. "I've never thought of you as being one of those abused women who couldn't shake off her abuser."

She stared at him with an anemic look for a very long time. "No, but I also cared about his sister. Then once the blackmail started—"

"*Blackmail?*" Aiden pounced.

"And everything I tell you will just make it seem very much like I *did* kill him," she protested, turning to address Aiden.

"If we take that off the board," Aiden suggested, "maybe it will help me understand what's going on here. So, how about we just start with the truth?"

She sank deeper into her seat, marshaling her thoughts. "He had a sister, … has a sister."

"Okay," Aiden replied calmly. "What does she have to do with this?"

"She's the only reason I went back to him," she explained, "and only because he blackmailed me, saying that he'd leave her alone if I came back."

"Leave her alone? How?"

"In every way possible," she stated. "I don't think he sexually abused her, but I know he mentally and emotionally abused her. Everything he ever did has her waking up in the middle of the night, screaming in terror. He was probably always this kind of an asshole, but I can't be sure."

"Hang on a minute," Aiden said. "Let's get back to the beginning of your relationship with this guy."

"Fine. We were besties in high school, and I got very close with his sister, but then I decided to leave and go to a community college with some grant money—only he followed me there. I couldn't stay because he was ..." She stopped and frowned. "I guess the term is abusive."

"What do you mean, *you guess?*" Mountain asked, almost growling.

Aiden immediately put up his hand and glared at Mountain.

Mountain subsided. "Did he hit you?"

"No, not ..." She hesitated. "That would have been a clear-cut sign that I was in trouble. Still that doesn't mean I would have listened to anybody or would have seen these early warning signals because, hey, I was young and stupid and knew everything, right? Isn't that how the world works?"

At that, she glanced over apologetically at Mountain. "You were right. I mean, Moscow was an asshole. I didn't understand how bad things had gotten, but I was trying to save Michelle," she explained, "and I think the opposite has happened. He threatened to kill her if I didn't marry him, and he said he would blame that murder on me too."

"Whoa." Aiden let out a deep breath. "Back up, back up."

She nodded. "I managed to get away from him for a couple years. I don't even know where he went during that time period. I think he went back East for a while. Michelle was in a special group home, and she seemed really happy. I saw her on a regular basis, even though I no longer had anything to do with him. She's very sweet," Toby explained, "and I don't have any other family I care to have anything to do with."

"Including me," Mountain added, with another growl.

She shook her head. "No, not you. However, if I didn't do what you said immediately, then I wasn't taking your advice, and I felt ostracized."

He just stared at her and shook his head. "I didn't mean it that way."

"I know, but I took it that way." She looked over at Aiden and continued her story. "Anyway, for a couple years, everything was fine. About four, maybe five years ago, he came back to town. He wanted to pick up where we left off, but where we left off was a bad place, and I didn't want to get back into that scenario. Yet he realized that I was seeing his sister on a regular basis, and he used that against me. He told me that, if I wanted to continue to see her, I would have to play nice. I told him that I didn't want anything to do with him, other than being friends, but that was it. So, if it came down to leaving his sister to get Moscow out of my life, then I would walk away from his sister." Toby shook her head. "I hated to do it, but I didn't know what else to do. He then turned around and told his sister that."

"Wow. Nice guy."

"No, not very much," she countered. "At this point in time, that stalemate lasted for a while. I stayed away from Michelle, until his sister called me one day, asking for help. She said the cops wouldn't help her, and she had nobody else who she could turn to."

"And why didn't *you* call the police?" Aiden asked.

"We don't deal well with the police in our family," she murmured. "My father runs a casino, and, I mean, I won't say he does it illegally, but I won't say that the law looks on him kindly either."

"And so you think that, if you had phoned the police, you would have gotten the same kind of response that Michelle had gotten?"

"I think so, yes," Toby agreed. "No, I don't know that for sure. I also didn't know if anybody would even believe Michelle because I wasn't sure I even believed her because of her disability. Whenever she would describe what was going on, she often couldn't get the words out. So I had to talk to Moscow. I finally ended up—over weeks of talking to him—realizing that he was threatening to take her away from the home where she was. I don't know if it was due to costs or was just his mind games. Like I told you, he wasn't a very nice guy. The bottom line? She felt like her life was in danger."

"How?" Aiden asked.

"Again we're dealing with somebody with a disability," she repeated, "and that just adds to the problem here."

AIDEN NODDED SLOWLY. He didn't have very much experience dealing with this particular health aspect. Yet he could imagine that would definitely lead to some extenuating circumstances, where life would become quite difficult, where they could perceive a threat when, maybe, there wasn't one. He waited for Toby to continue. "And …"

She nodded. "So I talked to Moscow and asked him what was going on, and he said it was none of my business and to butt out. He had already contacted the home and had told them that I was to have no access to Michelle, in person or on the phone. However, Michelle contacted me again and again. It became a worry and then a nuisance." She raised both palms. "And I'll admit that I didn't think very much of myself when I realized that Michelle really did have a legitimate problem, and I was pushing her off because I couldn't deal," she explained, "so that made me feel like I was a terrible person as well."

"Of course," Mountain agreed calmly, "and you didn't have anybody you felt you could ask for help."

"No," she confirmed. "If you'd been around, I would have asked you, but it was pretty hard to even get a hold of you there for a while."

At that, he winced and nodded. "It often still is," he shared, "and part of the problem is, who *did* you talk to?"

"I tried to talk to my mother about it once, but she got quite angry that I was even involved in something like that and told me that it was a bad deal and that I should just step out of it."

"Well, gee, what a surprise," Mountain quipped. At Aiden's look, Mountain explained to him, "Toby's mom has a habit of not dealing with anything that's unpleasant. If it will upset anybody, especially her, she won't get involved."

"Even if Michelle was being hurt?" Aiden asked.

Mountain shook his head. "Toby's mom won't have anything to do with it. Even if Toby herself were getting hurt. It won't matter. Toby's ma likes her grand conflict-free lifestyle. Everything else is a moot point."

Aiden looked over at Toby for confirmation, and she nodded. "Hate to say that," she noted, "but he's right. My mother doesn't like anything unpleasant. My father too. He works hard to keep all that conflict away from my mother."

"Okay. That's an interesting scenario," Aiden stated.

"Well, whether it is or not," she replied, "it's the family. Keeping the cops off Dad's back is pretty important to him. He also loves keeping things quiet and not making any ripples. He told me not to get involved in anything that would cause issues."

"Okay. Interesting again," Aiden noted. "You would think that somebody would have cared about Michelle's plight, as she's an innocent and not able to deal with this herself."

"I thought so too," Toby agreed, "but I was wrong. Nobody cared. I did eventually go to the police, and they ran a cursory check, *blah, blah, blah*, and found nothing is wrong."

"Of course. And psychological abuse is very hard to prove anyway," Aiden added. "In this case, it would be even worse."

"Exactly." Toby nodded. "So, I tried to keep her happy and to talk with her to see whether anything specific ever came out of her. By this time, after all the fuss I raised, Moscow allowed me to see Michelle, the once-a-week type thing. It became our Friday night adventure, but there just didn't seem to be anything to worry about, so I let it drop for the next few months. At this point in time, Moscow was kind of in and out of town, but I didn't really see him. Then she called me recently in the middle of the night, and she was bawling her eyes out." Toby pinched the bridge of her nose and took a deep breath.

"And no one cared. The home was dealing with multiple special-needs people there, so this was just a very exhausting scenario for me. I didn't want to try and push Michelle away or to dissuade her from her fears, but I didn't know what to do about it. Anyway, long story short is that Michelle finally told me that Moscow would come to the group home and would stand at the end of her bed in the middle of the night and just terrify her.

"When I asked the home whether anybody was allowed visitors at that hour, they replied no, that absolutely no way would something like that be allowed to happen. So I immediately assumed—incorrectly as it turns out—that Michelle was making it up. And, no, I don't mean she was making it up because she was trying to cause trouble. She's not like that. Yet this was something that was ongoing, and she was trying to deal with it.

"The trouble was, she couldn't deal with it, and the home wanted to talk about changing her medication and doing all kinds of stuff, so I backed off because I didn't want to cause Michelle any more trouble. I was at work one day—about six months ago—when Moscow came to my table and said, 'I'm somebody important around here, and you better behave yourself or else.' I just stared at him and then ignored him. It's not as if I hadn't heard those kinds of bullying taunts before from him. Besides, I was at work and not exactly free to talk. As it was, Moscow had interfered with the game enough that I got reprimanded for it."

She hesitated then added, "Finally Moscow caught me at home and told me that he wanted me back in his life. I said, 'No, that's not happening.' I wasn't that stupid and sure as hell wouldn't get back into a scenario that made me very unhappy. He told me that the only way he would stop tormenting his sister was if I got involved with him again. I tried to get more information out of him to find out exactly what he was doing to Michelle, but he wouldn't talk to me at all. He just told me that I knew what the deal was.

"Then I went back to his sister to talk to her some more. By now she wasn't saying much, but she'd lost a ton of weight. She was scared all the time. I'd take her out for ice cream, but she would always look around the corner, as if waiting to be pounced on. One time Moscow did come up to us while we were having ice cream, and she started screaming at the top of her lungs, and she had to be taken to the hospital and sedated. When I asked him what the hell that was all about, he just smiled and said that he needed to prove a point."

She stopped and stared at Aiden. "If that doesn't tell you what kind of an asshole he is, I don't know what would convince you."

Aiden frowned in shock. "And the cops didn't do any-thing?"

"Of course not," she snapped. "There still wasn't any-thing happening in their minds that was criminal." Aiden winced at that. She added, "Of course they still had caseloads upon caseloads of other types of criminals who were proba-bly something they could deal with, and poor Michelle's case would have been more of a family court thing—or a com-pletely different department than the clear-cut ones these cops would have been working on." She shook her head.

"One day," she added, "Moscow found me at the end of my workday and demanded that, if I didn't marry him right now, he would fix it so Michelle never got to sleep or would spend the rest of her life as this drugged-up vegetable. You've got to remember she was basically like a kid sister to me. We'd spent a lot of time together. I had avoided other relationships because I didn't want anything like what I'd previously experienced with Moscow," she explained, with a grimace, staring off in the distance.

"I told him 'Hell no,' and I went to the cops. Of course they went to him and talked to him, but he just laughed and told them it was absolutely nothing like that and told them about his sister's history and how she had this ability to twist things around. So, of course, the cops had the previous reports on file, and they also had a thick medical file on Michelle. So everything supported Moscow's version, not mine. He came back to me and basically put the boot to me," she stated calmly. "And, yes"—she looked over at her cousin—"that's the one and only time he laid a hand on me."

At that, Mountain jumped to his feet.

She shook her head. "He's dead. You can't kill him."

"Why the hell would you marry him if you knew that was coming?"

"Because, at that point in time," she explained, "I'd already been beaten up pretty good, and believe me. Not one visible scar was anywhere, so I told Moscow that the only way that I would go through with the deed was if he never touched me again in any way, shape, or form. It would be a marriage in name only because he really just wanted a possession. He was to leave his sister 100 percent alone, never see or torment her again, and to keep covering all Michelle's medical costs. He laughed and told me that I was a fool, and that nothing would ever change if I didn't marry him. And yet, even marrying him, he wouldn't guarantee anything. So then I said, 'Fine. In that case I'm not having anything to do with this.'"

Mountain nodded approvingly.

She grimaced and added, "Until his sister called me again, and I went to the home right away. Michelle had supposedly fallen down the stairs, but she kept saying that her brother had beaten her up."

"And you believed her."

"This time I believed her because I was still sporting the same kind of bruises myself," she noted. "The only reason I'm telling you this is so that you understand why we got married in Vegas a few days later. I had practically lived at the hospital, looking after Michelle. Once the hospital released her, she would return to the same group home, but she was heavily medicated and not doing very well. I guess, in retrospect, the damage had already been done, and I was probably a fool to think I could do anything to stave off more. But Moscow ushered me right into one of the little chapels on the strip," she said. "We got married very quickly, without any fanfare or any romance—which was good because it was all I could do to get the words *I do* choked out of me.

"And just as we stepped outside the chapel, he looked at me and smiled and said, 'Now I promise I'll spend the rest of my life making this worthwhile.' Yet I already knew it was a horrible mistake and was trying to figure out how to get the hell out of this when a vehicle drove up with a couple guys in it. They hauled Moscow away in the vehicle and left me standing there on the strip. I headed back to my house, not sure what had just gone on, but I wasn't too worried, as Moscow had greeted them like buddies.

"Matter of fact, I felt relieved, escaping from whatever he had planned to come. I went to bed that night with the doors and windows locked. I checked up on Michelle the next morning, and she was doing much better. She was still medicated, and I went to work. I saw no sign of Moscow that day or the next, and I started to think that maybe, just maybe, he'd run off. Maybe he had this weird psychosis and just wanted to show he had that power over me, and maybe he had just buggered off. Of course, you know, that was way too much to hope for." She shrugged.

"Later I look up from my table, and my boss is coming toward me, and the cops are with him. I was immediately told that Moscow was dead. His body had showed up in a Dumpster down the road. I was shocked. I sure wasn't grieving. In fact, it was the opposite. I was almost elated because I had desperately wanted to get out of this sham marriage but didn't know how, and the cops didn't like my reaction," she noted.

"And did you explain?"

"Of course not. How do you explain something like that?" she murmured. "I wasn't even sure how to explain it to myself. I mean, it's just too stupid—all of it is. I should never have married him, but, at the same time, I didn't know how to stop his abuse of Michelle."

"Somebody like that," Aiden noted, "has learned a long time ago what works. So, from his perspective, he could manipulate you the same way he did his sister."

She nodded. "And I get that. I really wish that I'd never met him in high school. I wish I had never seen him again," she said. "He's a vile nightmare, and I'm still paying."

"And why would the cops think that you killed him?" Aiden asked.

"I am not exactly sure that I have an answer for that," she replied. "Honestly I think I looked good for it, and they stopped looking elsewhere. Still, Moscow had a lot of enemies."

Mountain interrupted. "Surely there would have been a lot of really good suspects."

"I heard Moscow had something in his pocket," she relayed, with a headshake. "Something that supposedly implicated me—a note with my name and a bank account number. But I don't know anything about that bank account. We didn't have any accounts in common, and, according to the police, a lot of money is in it, and, because we're legally married, then that money becomes mine. Of course, to them, that's my motive. Obviously I have a lot of reasons to get married and to turn around and kill him, but they didn't know the whole truth. But they did know that I wasn't upset about his death. In truth I was delighted."

"And, of course," Aiden noted, "you were afraid that, by telling the truth, you would put another nail in your coffin."

"Exactly," she confirmed. "And now you know what happened. The cops are looking at motive. It's almost always the partner. I'm the new wife. I have a lot of motive for getting rid of him. If I tell them that he beat me up and forced me to marry him and that he's been abusing his sister, all that ever does is give the cops more motivation and more reason to see me as the best murder suspect they have."

"Right," Aiden agreed. "The tangled webs we weave."

She snorted. "Some of us didn't weave any of them," she muttered. "Some of us just tried hard to live a life and to befriend a damaged young lady, yet become ensnared anyway."

"And the four other murders they're trying to pin on you?"

"You know what? I think, as far as the cops are concerned, as soon as they got me on the one, they were looking at all their unsolved case files," she guessed, "and wondered if they could pigeonhole me into those too."

"And apparently there was a connection?" Aiden asked her.

"Yes." She nodded. "There definitely was a connection, with me being a dealer at a casino, and all four of these guys had won some big money."

"Interesting." Aiden stared at her.

She shrugged. "I don't think 'interesting' is quite the word I would use."

"Did you know any of the men personally?"

"Personally?" She hesitated, then slowly shook her head. "I just know them from my table."

"And were they all killed before your husband?"

She flinched at the term *husband*. "I don't know. I mean, their bodies were all found recently. However, I have no idea in what order they were murdered."

"So, what's to stop the cops from thinking that your husband killed the others?" Aiden asked Toby.

She looked at him, frowning.

"Those murders could be the source of the money in that account," Aiden explained, "the money that you don't know anything about."

She stared at him. "That never occurred to me." Then she looked over at her cousin. "I'm not sure if the cops considered that."

"We'll get to the bottom of that," Mountain promised. "Where were the bodies found?"

"The cops told me they were all in Dumpsters."

"All of them?"

She nodded. "So that's another connection right there."

"And the problem with that is," Mountain added, "you're not strong enough to lift any man and drop him into a Dumpster, are you?"

# CHAPTER 2

"**Y**OU KNOW THAT it's always been a bone of contention in my life that I'm five-ten and weigh 110 pounds. I might be physically fit, but lifting up Moscow?" she asked, with a headshake. "Not happening. He's fit. He's a gym buff and big."

"Your husband?" Aiden confirmed.

She nodded slowly. "I really, really, *really* hate that term."

"The good news is," Aiden replied, "you're no longer married because you're now a widow."

"Thank God for that too," she said, then came a bitter laugh. "And, of course, if the cops hear me say that, you know what'll happen."

"First off," Aiden stated, "you've already been charged for his murder. Do you have a lawyer on retainer?"

She shook her head. "No, I was hoping to get a public defender. I can't even believe I need to do this."

"Fine," Aiden replied, "and what lawyer would that be?"

"I don't know. I know Dad is not footing the bill." She snorted, looking over at Mountain.

Mountain shook his head. "Of course not. It's all about keeping his nose clean, isn't it? His daughter gets charged with murder, and it's got nothing to do with him."

"That's about the size of it," she agreed. "And I'm sure

my mother has already lost my phone number."

Mountain winced. "And your sister?"

"Same as my mother, you know that."

"Did they know Moscow?"

"They loved him. He was charming and good-looking, wore suits well, played at the casinos and apparently won," she explained, with a shrug. "That's all that mattered to them. It's all about appearances and money."

"Lovely family," Aiden said, shaking his head. He looked over at Mountain. "Have you got anything to add to this?"

"Moscow is a fucking asshole," Mountain declared. "I tore into her pretty good when I heard she was back with him. She didn't explain about Michelle though."

"You didn't give me a chance," she stated, glaring at him.

He thought about it and nodded. "You could be right, and, for that, I'm sorry."

She shrugged. "You know what happens when you start this downward slide. It all goes really fast."

"It can," Mountain murmured, "but it doesn't have to be all bad."

"Really? Feels like it's all bad."

He nodded slowly. "For that, I'm sorry again. I never intended to desert you."

"Nobody *intends* on deserting anybody."

Aiden spoke up. "Maybe one of the questions right now that I need to ask is, How is Michelle?"

She turned toward Aiden, smiled, and replied, "She's doing better. She does seem to understand that her brother is dead. Since then, she's started sleeping again."

"That sounds like pretty good proof right there that Moscow was tormenting her," he murmured.

"Believe me. Nobody gives a shit about the proof. All the cops care about is whether they can make a case and can put somebody away for it. And I'm not sure why my parents hired you guys."

At that, Aiden frowned and looked over at Mountain. "That's what Corbin said."

Mountain nodded. "I think so. I'll check on that."

"You do that," she said, "because I can't imagine that ever happening, which is one of the reasons why I'm really confused as to why you're here."

Aiden thought about it. "Regardless of why I am here, I will look into your case."

"What if you get another call for another case? Will you dump me too?" He looked at her. She sighed. "Sorry, I'm not trying to be a bitch."

"I think, after everything you've been through, you're entitled to have some strong emotions."

She stared at him, her lips quirking. "*Strong emotions?* Obviously you're one of those nice guys."

"Which you don't like apparently."

"I got rid of the bad guys as much as I could," she countered. "Believe me. It's not all that easy when they're real shits."

"No," Aiden replied, "you're right. I kind of like the idea of Moscow being responsible for the four other deaths."

"You know what? The only thing wrong with that is I can't really see it because he's the kind of guy who doesn't like to get his hands dirty."

"Well, he got his hands dirty when he attacked you and Michelle, didn't he?"

"But I can't prove it," she said. "What I do know is the cops think I did murder Moscow." Her doorbell rang. She groaned. "And that, I think, is the lawyer."

"Why would he come to your house?" Mountain queried, immediately bouncing to his feet.

She stared at him. "Don't they?"

"No," Aiden replied gently, "generally they don't."

She got up, walked to the front door, and, just as she went to open it, Mountain grabbed her and said, "No." And he pulled her back.

AIDEN HOPPED UP, put himself between the two of them, and guided her back to the living room. Mountain opened the front door and slipped outside.

"What's that all about?" she asked, glaring at him.

"Your cousin is just checking to make sure who's at the door."

Her shoulders sagged. "I don't know why he's worried about me now."

"We're here because he cares about you," Aiden stated. "I don't know if he hired the Mavericks himself or if he pulled some strings and made it so or that your father did this. I don't know. I do know Mountain won't like it if you interfere with us doing our jobs here."

She looked up at him and nodded slowly. "You do know him, don't you?" But a wry tone filled her voice.

"I know a lot about him. I know the things that matter. And I know that he's here to help you out."

She sighed and sat down again. "I can't imagine that anybody can do anything with this mess."

"The authorities need to have more than just a dead body and a motive in order to put you on the hot seat."

"I have been charged," she noted. "I've posted bail, and I tell you what. Nothing like realizing this is happening in your world and you can do nothing to stop it."

"It's also the kind of stuff we do," Aiden told her.

She shook her head. "No, that's not the kind of stuff you do."

He chuckled. "Okay," he agreed, "it's similar to stuff we do."

"Maybe," she relented, and then she yawned.

He looked at her and asked, "Are you getting any sleep at night?"

She shook her head. "How does one sleep when you understand that your life as you know it is passing you by, and, before you have any inkling of what's going on, you know that you'll get through some sort of a monkey trial and will end up in jail for years and years?" she asked. "I didn't do anything but try to protect a young woman who was being tormented by her brother. And yet I couldn't even seem to do that properly."

"You did what you could," he murmured. "Don't ever feel bad about that. Obviously, if you'd had some help, it would have been a lot easier."

"I've been concerned about her for a long time. I know she's doing better and that's good, but…" She looked up at him. "I'd hate to see her slide back again."

"Sure." He shrugged. "Nobody should have to deal with that kind of torture. Dealing with it takes time."

"He was really good at it," she noted. "He always just kept to the side of the law."

"Not once he laid a hand on you and Michelle."

"Yeah, and yet who would I tell? It's not as if my father wanted to know or my mother gave a shit, and it's not as if the cops wanted anything to do with it even after I'd already been to them a couple times asking for help for Michelle. To them, it was just a *cry wolf* scenario."

"Only this time, it was you and not Michelle."

"Exactly. One cop even went so far as to say that I was just making it all up."

"Of course. Did Moscow have a good reputation in town?"

"Oh, he did." She nodded. "He had lots of friends. I mean, if he'd lived, he might very well have ended up with some political career. He was definitely slimy."

"Those guys often have great political careers," he said, with a laugh.

She nodded. "And his father is also a big man in town."

"That's another thing that's probably driving this investigation in your direction."

"Sure. He hates me. I'm nothing but a casino girl who hooked his fantastic son and ruined his life."

"Wow. And what about his mentally challenged daughter?"

"I don't think he acknowledges her at all." She sighed. "Just another broken-family issue. Technically Michelle is his stepdaughter. She's not his by blood. Moscow's birth parents split when Moscow was four, and his mom remarried, and that's when she had Michelle."

"Right. So, as far as Moscow's father is concerned, the stepsister's got nothing to do with him."

"Exactly. And most people say those mental health issues have nothing to do with them, as in the genes or whatever. Michelle has a lot of mental health issues, if that's even what it is called. Supposedly she has a chromosome issue," Toby explained. "Michelle is one of the sweetest, nicest ladies I've ever met, and I really love her. And I'm so sorry for everything that happened to her, even though I tried so hard to stop it."

"And you have to stop feeling guilty about that too." Aiden frowned. "The good news is, your husband is dead. So neither of you have to go through that torment any longer."

Her shoulders sagged.

He looked at her closely, leaned forward, and asked, "Or are you grieving him?"

She stared at him in shock, shook her head immediately. "No, not at all, but getting over his abuse takes time," she declared. "But Michelle? I can't be sure that she isn't mourning or grieving his loss."

"Not likely," Aiden guessed. "At the same time, it doesn't matter because this is something that needs to be dealt with now."

She nodded. "I don't think she understands." She looked over at the door. "Why hasn't Mountain returned?"

"Do you want me to go check?"

She frowned and shook her head. "No. I'm not on house arrest. I can get up and leave, but, once they decide I'm guilty," she stated bitterly, "I can't go visit Michelle anymore."

The fact that she was so concerned about Michelle warmed Aiden's heart. At the same time, he had no idea what kind of mental state Michelle was in after all this torture. And who knows? Maybe there was a better avenue for her than this. "Have you ever thought about whether she'd be better off without you as a reminder?"

"Yes," she admitted, looking at him. "I have, and I did talk to the psychologist about it and to Michelle's counselors. But every time she sees me, she gives me such a big smiling welcome that it made them feel I was helping her to heal."

"That's good," he noted.

"Well, it's good, but it's also rough," she murmured, "because she often asks me questions that I can't answer."

"Like what?"

She stared at him for a long moment. "She saw the bruises on me. She's always asking me where he is and if we're safe."

"*Hmm,*" he replied. "I guess, in her mind, she can't quite reconcile that you are both safe now."

"No, I don't think so. She has been told that he's dead, but I don't know if she gets it."

"Hopefully," he added, "at least over time, they should help her with that at the home. Plus further counseling."

At that, Mountain returned. "It's the cops."

She groaned. "Now what?"

"They found another body," he told her.

"What? And, because I'm out on bail, I'm a suspect?"

"Absolutely. You're a suspect, and I'm letting them in so that they can talk to you."

She stared at him, wordless. Then the words burst from her. "How is that helping me?"

He gave her a hard look. "You'll tell them everything, including where you were last night."

"I was here alone," she said. "How am I supposed to have an alibi for something that I didn't know I would need one for?"

And, of course, that was always a problem, as Aiden knew from other cases. Given a choice, everybody would have an alibi. But, in her case, she didn't have anybody to stay with her. Aiden would make that change right here and now.

As the cops came in to join them, they looked at her and then at Aiden. He nodded to them. "Good afternoon."

They frowned at her and stated, "We need to speak with you."

"Fine," she replied. "Go ahead. No reason my cousin and Aiden can't hear what you want to know."

They looked at Aiden and asked, "When did you arrive in town?"

"Both of us came in this morning," he said easily, knowing the cops would check the flight info. "We haven't been here long, so she has no alibi for last night. Again, she didn't know she needed one."

"Of course." One of the cops snorted.

"So, what's your evidence that she has anything to do with these cases?" Mountain asked, leaning against the door. Just his size was intimidating, but he did try to stand back ever-so-slightly, so as not to crowd the cops and to make them look like he was in their space.

"You're Mountain, aren't you?" the lead cop asked suddenly, looking at him.

He frowned. "Yeah. Do I know you?"

"You sure do." He reached out a hand. "We went to school together."

Mountain stared at him. "Ben? Ben Rosco?"

The cop nodded. "Yeah, that's me." He looked over at Toby. "Are you related to her?"

"She's my cousin," Mountain said, staring at him.

That news seemed to make him swallow. "You'll make life difficult for us, won't you?"

"If you charge her with something which I know she didn't do, like you've charged her with murder, of course I will. How can I not?" As he looked pointedly over at the other cop, he added, "And Ben knows me well enough to understand that, if I say she didn't do it, she didn't do it."

"But you also know that we've got to follow up all leads," the second cop stated doggedly.

At that, Mountain turned to the lead cop again. "Ben, you know she didn't do it."

"I don't know that," Ben argued, glaring at Mountain, trying hard to stay neutral.

"Whatever," Toby snapped from the couch. "Ask your questions. The only way you find out who *really* did this is when you're done focusing on me."

"Considering that they've already charged you," Mountain explained, "that's hardly likely."

The second cop looked nervous. "Still, following up all leads."

"If you've charged her, it means that you're only looking to secure who you already have as a suspect," Mountain declared, looking over at his cousin. "Like she said, ask your questions."

"Well, what we wanted to know first off is where you were last night," Ben said, "between midnight and four a.m."

"Here, sleeping," she stated instantly. "And, like Aiden told you, I have no alibi because I sleep alone." At that, the men looked at her steadily. She raised an eyebrow. "Yes, I sleep alone, and I have done so for a very long time."

"What about your husband?" Ben asked in a delicate voice.

She snorted. "You won't believe any of what I say anyway," she said.

Ben looked down at his notes. "Do you know this man?" he asked, holding up a photo.

She looked at him and nodded. "He's a regular at my

table."

"At your table?"

"He is a regular at the casino," she corrected. "I have no idea where the customers go when they're not at my table. For all I know, they hit all the tables in all the casinos. That's not uncommon."

Aiden knew that a lot of people who went to the casinos were really diehard gamblers, but that didn't mean they stuck with the same dealer or that they didn't come back hours later to a different dealer on the next shift or to a different game. Aiden stepped around and looked at the picture. "Pretty nondescript too, isn't he?" he asked in a conversational tone. "Probably what? Five-ten, longer brown hair, maybe brown eyes, thin medium build, nothing very discerning about him."

At that, the two cops stared at him, and Ben asked, "What's that got to do with it?"

Aiden shrugged. "Presumably you have a positive ID on the victim?"

Ben nodded. "Yes. This is John Brown."

At the name, he raised an eyebrow. "Is that a legit name?"

"It is, apparently," Ben stated. "Regardless, he's dead. He was found in a Dumpster, same as the others."

Her shoulders slumped at that.

"That upsets you?" Ben asked her.

"I was hoping," she added, "that my late husband would have been the killer and that you would find that out and that I would be off the hook."

The two cops stared at her. "What?"

"I didn't kill any of these men, so somebody else did. And, if somebody else did, knowing my ex, I would say that he would be a likely candidate. But the fact is, he is dead, so he didn't kill this latest victim."

"And why would your husband have killed any of them?" Ben queried.

"Because I don't know what he did for a living. I don't believe he had any visible means of support, outside of gambling. These dead guys all should have had money on them that they recently won from the games," she noted. "For all I know, these were robberies."

The men wrote down a couple notes. Mountain stepped forward and cleared his throat, but she just glared at him. Aiden immediately placed a hand on her shoulder and murmured, "Tell them."

"They won't believe me anyway."

"But, if you tell them, then it's in the record that you've done what you can do."

Her shoulders slumped again, and she glared at him. "You know you guys can leave anytime too."

"Wouldn't that be nice?" Aiden quipped, smiling down at her. "However, that won't happen."

She turned and looked at the cops.

"What's going on?" Ben asked.

"She didn't tell you all the story because she doesn't feel like you guys will believe her."

"That won't happen," Ben argued.

"What we do believe happened," Mountain began, "is that you already have a murder suspect locked in and that you're not looking at anybody else."

"That's not true," Ben protested, as he looked over at his partner, who stared at Mountain uneasily. "Look. If she's got something to help clear her, we need to know," Ben said.

"And again she doesn't feel like you'll believe her,"

Mountain repeated.

"Which doesn't matter. Yet, if she's lied on her statement, that's already one lie we've caught her in."

"Exactly what we're hearing from you right there is why she's uncomfortable speaking with you two," Mountain stated. "So I guess the only answer is for her lawyer to get here pretty soon, and then you cops can talk to him. She has already asked for a public defender, but I hired her a lawyer," Mountain shared gently.

Toby's jaw dropped.

"And don't even begin to argue with me," Mountain told her. "When you're getting railroaded, it's important that somebody is in your corner. … I've always been in your corner, whether you believe it or not."

Aiden smiled. "There you go. Now we're getting somewhere." He looked over at the cops. "She'll talk to her lawyer, and then she can come down and talk to you guys, if the lawyer believes it's important."

The cops didn't like that obviously, but they had no reason to haul her down to the station. They nodded slowly, got up to leave, and Ben added, "You're not leaving town, are you?"

"It's a provision of my bail," she snapped in a hard tone, "something that you guys made sure you accused me of right away."

Ben looked over at Mountain. "You know it's a pretty good case."

"It's a bullshit case," Mountain snapped. "Don't think we don't know who Moscow's father is."

At that, the second cop had the grace to look ashamed.

"Look," Ben said. "She still gets a fair shake. We'll obviously not railroad her into a murder trial if she didn't do the crime."

"She *didn't* do the crime," Mountain repeated calmly, "but I highly doubt you'll change anything about what you're doing in the next little while, until we find some *real* evidence."

They didn't like hearing that either. As they headed to the door, Ben looked at Aiden and asked, "Where are you staying?"

"I'm staying here," he replied cheerfully. "She'll have an alibi for every night from here on."

They didn't like hearing that either.

"So, if you get another victim," Aiden explained, "make sure you come and check on her whereabouts."

And, with that, the two cops left quickly.

She looked over at Aiden. "Are you serious?"

"Absolutely. They can't do anything if you're cleared. It's all bullshit anyway, and it's politically driven."

"That's obvious," she agreed. "That doesn't get me off the hook though."

"No, but finding the truth does," Aiden declared, looking over at Mountain. "What's your take on it?"

"Same as yours. The cops don't have any suspects. Toby looks good for it. And her father-in-law wants it to look even better."

"So, do you think the cops have some fabricated evidence?" Aiden asked.

Mountain nodded. "I wouldn't be at all surprised."

Just then came another ring of the doorbell.

She groaned. "I can go weeks to months without anybody stopping in," she shared. "Now apparently I'm popular."

"Nope," Mountain stated. "This should be your lawyer."

She glared at him, but he disappeared. She looked over at Aiden. "He didn't have to hire me a lawyer."

"He did," Aiden disagreed, looking at her, "and you'll accept this and say *Thank you very much* with a smile on your face."

"And if I don't?"

"You'll break his heart," Aiden murmured, before Mountain had a chance to come back. "He's doing everything he can to help you out. You might want to let other people step in and give you a little bit of assistance. He feels bad enough that he couldn't help you before."

She continued to stare at Aiden, but then the new arrival was here. And this time it was definitely a lawyer. He wore a three-piece suit and carried the prerequisite briefcase, but it was the look on his face, that hawk look that said he scented something of interest.

The lawyer focused on her, nodded slowly, and stated, "I've been at your table."

"Sure," she agreed, studying him. "I remember you."

"I have never seen you cheat at the table," he noted.

"Because I don't cheat," she said immediately. "It's a pretty good way to lose your job."

He nodded. "I can imagine that. … Got yourself in a spot of trouble."

"Well, *Vegas* has got a spot of trouble," Aiden argued defensively. "In case you didn't know that there's been now six murders in the last week, including Moscow's."

At that, the lawyer turned toward him. "Seriously?"

Mountain corrected him. "A couple were earlier," he noted, "so make them all within two weeks."

"Jesus!" the lawyer exclaimed. "How come that hasn't been public news?"

"Because they're pinning all of them on my cousin," Mountain stated, "with a couple major facts that don't fit."

"Let's start at the beginning," the lawyer said. He placed a recorder on the coffee table. "Now tell me what the hell's going on."

# CHAPTER 3

---

TOBY WAS EXHAUSTED by the time she told the lawyer everything.

He stared her down and asked, "Do they have any evidence?"

Mountain shook his head. "None that the cops are willing to tell us about. None they've asked her about. They don't have camera feeds. They don't have anything along that line. The only thing they have is motive."

"And possibly a good motive," the attorney agreed, with a nod. "Nothing like the beaten wife syndrome to make people angry."

"They don't even know about that though," she said.

He looked over at her. "What?"

"That's the thing. I knew they wouldn't believe me in the first place, so I didn't tell them. The couple times I've gone in and talked to them about Moscow's possible abuse of my sister-in-law, they've run me off as being a kook, making up stories."

At that, she had to tell her lawyer about Michelle too. When Toby finally ran dry, she looked up to see Aiden standing there, offering her a glass of water. She took it gratefully, wondering at this man who saw things like that and who stepped in to take care of issues. She hadn't ever had anybody look after her all these years. It felt weird now.

She looked at her lawyer. "So I didn't tell them because I knew they would say I just made it all up."

"Do you have anything documented?"

She frowned, as she thought about it. "I didn't go to the hospital. I didn't go to the police, so I guess the answer is no."

"Do you have any pictures?"

"You know what? My friend from work might," she added. "Annabel works at the casino with me. I was in the ladies' room, trying to fix a broken bra strap, when she saw my back. I know she snapped a photo."

Aiden immediately hopped up and asked, "What's her name and phone number?"

When Toby hesitated, he added, "Look. Even if she won't talk to you, leave a message, telling her that you're sending somebody over. She could send you the photo otherwise. And, if she doesn't want to talk to you, I'll go have a private talk with her myself." No threat was in his voice, but that tone meant he'd get the job done.

The lawyer looked at Aiden in alarm.

Mountain smiled. "Hey, it's better that he goes versus me. I'd make damn sure I got that photo," he stated. "Aiden will do it nicely enough."

The lawyer rolled his eyes. "Don't do anything to jeopardize her case."

She picked up the phone and called her friend. When Annabel answered, Toby identified herself.

"Oh, my God. Is it true? Did you kill him?"

"No, I didn't kill him." Toby pinched the bridge of her nose. "You know that."

"Jesus. Yeah, yet you know, I wondered," she said in that conciliatory voice. "Had to ask."

"Look. A while back you took that photo of my back, after my late husband beat me up."

"Yeah, I remember," she replied.

"Do you still have that photo?"

"I didn't take it off my phone, so I should," she answered.

"Could you send it to me?"

"Sure," she said, then she hesitated. "Am I allowed to?"

"Yes, you're allowed to share a photo of me with me," Toby explained in a dry tone. "The cops don't believe that Moscow ever touched me."

"Jesus. He beat the crap out of you that day," she replied. "Don't worry, hon. I'm sending it to you right now. If you need anything else, let me know." With that, Annabel rang off.

The guys looked over at her. "That was fast."

She shrugged. "Probably because she has to go to work." She checked the time on her phone. She nodded.

"I guess you don't have a job anymore," Aiden noted.

"Well, I do," she explained. "They gave me a few days off. Since my father is big in the industry, they have given me the benefit of a doubt, as long as it stays under the table. If there's any public outcry about it, then, yeah, I'm out."

"Interesting," Aiden replied.

At that, the lawyer laughed. "Not really. She's an extremely popular dealer, and people are always at her table."

She nodded. "And, for that reason alone, they'll probably allow me to keep my job, but how depressing to think that that would be the reason."

"It's all about money," the lawyer stated.

Her phone buzzed. She picked it up. "Looks like she sent it." It took a moment to download, and, when Toby brought it up, she winced and handed her phone to her lawyer.

He whistled slowly. "Jesus. He did this to you?"

She nodded. "Yes. The thing is," she stated, "I didn't kill Moscow or any of the others, and the cops'll just take this as further evidence of motive that I did."

He nodded. "It's more motive, which isn't good."

"Nope, it isn't," she agreed. "All I can tell you is that I didn't kill Moscow or the other guys."

"Also keep in mind," Mountain added, "that she isn't physically capable of lifting these guys up and throwing them in the Dumpsters."

The lawyer looked at him and then nodded. "So the cops will say she has an accomplice."

"Of course they'll say that," she groaned. "But they have to find them, don't they?"

"It depends on if somebody will pay them to take a fall and to blame you and to do a few years of jail time in order to get free and clear of other debts, say, like gambling debts," Mountain explained in a casual and calm and noncommittal voice.

She stared at him in shock. "Oh my God. Why would anybody do that?"

Aiden answered that. "To make sure that you get locked up for killing his son."

She stared at him and shook her head wildly. "But I didn't do it." Fear and panic started to set in, as she realized just how much people with money—like Moscow's father— could make her life impossible at this stage. She looked over at the lawyer. "You've got to believe me. I didn't kill any of them."

"I don't have to believe you," he replied, "but the police,

and, in a worst case scenario, the jury does."

At that, Mountain slammed his fist into the doorjamb and stepped outside. She looked over at Aiden, but he was looking at the picture on her phone.

"You want to send me a copy of that?" Aiden asked her.

She avoided looking at the photo and shrugged. "Sure. But what difference will it make?"

"I'm not sure, but you know that a father who thinks that this is okay doesn't sound like my kind of a man."

"Don't talk to him," the lawyer ordered Aiden immediately. "We can't have anything compromise her case."

"Nope. But maybe it's like father, like son," Aiden murmured. "Did you ever show your father this?"

She slowly shook her head. "How could I?" she asked. "I just got it from my friend."

"Sure. But did you let your parents see your body or any of the injuries Moscow caused?"

"No," she told him. "In my family, that was one of those things that you're not supposed to talk about. You're not supposed to be so stupid as to get beaten up by some guy. And remember. They idolized him. Moscow and my parents were all about appearances."

"Sure. But apparently not about appearances when it comes to beating the crap out of his wife."

"Well, I was only his girlfriend back then," she added. "Another reason why the cops won't believe me because I did marry him afterward. I'm still not even sure how that happened, but I was trying to save Michelle."

"And I don't think you told me about that either," the lawyer said, hitting the Record button. "Let's get back to it."

By the time she spilled all about this part, the attorney just stared at her in shock. She shrugged. "Michelle doesn't deserve any of this. She's been tormented enough by him. She's like real family to me. What was I supposed to do? The only thing I could think of was to marry him and to hope that he left me and Michelle alone."

The attorney shook his head. "With this kind of a bully and a budding sociopath, you know for a fact that would never happen."

"I had hoped it would," she stated, "because how would I help Michelle? Otherwise I would be completely lost."

"You *were* completely lost," the lawyer noted, "until somebody decided to save you."

At that, she stared at Aiden and whispered, "Yes, but at what cost? At what cost?"

AIDEN STEPPED OUT onto the deck, and, instead of wasting time on a text, he phoned Corbin. When he answered, Aiden quickly explained what was going on. "I need the case files for all six of these murders."

"Only six?" Corbin asked, with a note of humor. "What about the late husband?"

Aiden frowned. "I'm counting him too. I need everything on him. I need all the history you can find on him—everything. But, more than that, on his father too."

"Why his father?"

"Because he's a bigwig in town, and I think he's running this investigation against her."

"Well, that's not very smart," he noted. "She has family too."

"But they aren't standing up for her, outside of Mountain."

"And yet, according to my paperwork, her father hired us or got us involved."

"Yeah. I think if you dig a little deeper, you'll find that Mountain got us involved and is paying for this gig," he shared in a dry tone.

A moment of silence came at the other end. "Well, damn. He must feel pretty strongly about this."

"Yeah, I think so," Aiden confirmed. "He's also not talking very much."

"No, but that's Mountain. He'll reserve judgment until he is at a point in time where he thinks he has something to really talk about."

"Maybe. But it would help me not feel quite so frustrated if I had more information on this."

"Not a whole lot of information to be had yet," Corbin noted. "I can't even believe that the cops have charged her already."

"Neither can the lawyer. But, hey, you know that's why I think some railroading is going on."

"We'll get to the bottom of it, I'm sure," Corbin said. "I'll get back to you."

And just as he went to ring off, Aiden added, "I'll also stay here."

Then came another moment of silence. "Okay. Why?"

"Because whoever's killing all these guys," Aiden explained, "he's making sure he's doing it at a very quick pace. Already five are dead, with another one found just last night. She didn't have an alibi because nobody else lives here with her. So, I'm staying to make sure that, if there's yet another murder, I'm her alibi."

"Not bad," Corbin noted. "I don't like a lot about this."

"Yeah, don't worry," Aiden replied. "I don't like an awful lot about this either."

Corbin laughed. "Just mind your *P*s and *Q*s with Mountain."

Aiden snorted. "He and Toby are barely talking. So keeping out of trouble won't be easy."

"Oh, they're talking. They just have some history to sort through."

"Isn't that always the way?" Aiden said. "Anyway I missed lunch. Could use some food."

"You've got a budget," Corbin noted helpfully.

"Yeah. I don't really know that I want anybody knowing I'm here though," Aiden added.

"We can send something over. What do you want?"

"Pizza," he replied immediately.

Corbin snorted. "Seriously? All the food choices in the world in Vegas, and that's what you want?"

"Nobody will know or even think anything odd about pizza being delivered to her door," Aiden explained. "And, right now, quite a few people have been back-and-forth. So a pizza delivery would raise the least amount of alarms."

"Done." With that, Corbin was gone.

Aiden stepped back into the living room to see Toby in a deep conversation with her lawyer. Good. As long as she was talking to him, maybe she could tell him something that could help her case.

As Aiden sat down beside Toby, she frowned. He frowned right back. She groaned. "Why are you guys all the same?"

His eyes widened. "*Us* guys are always the same?" he asked politely.

She glared at him. "You know what I mean."

"Nope. Haven't a clue," he countered cheerfully. He

looked over at the lawyer. "Are you getting what you need?"

"Nothing to get," he admitted. "She has no alibi for any of these deaths, but the fact remains that she is not capable of doing this on her own, which also means the cops would just look for an accomplice."

Aiden nodded and turned toward her. "Who's in your closest circle?"

"Nobody," she stated bluntly. "Because of my ex, I stayed isolated, knowing that he would go after all of them."

"And I hate to ask," Aiden began, "because you've mentioned that Michelle has some issues, but would the cops look at her as being your accomplice?"

Toby stared at him in astonishment and then slowly shook her head. "Hell, the cops might look, but could they ever convict her over something like that?"

"That's not the point though," Aiden noted. "You know it's certainly happened in other cases where people have used someone just like Michelle."

Toby nodded slowly. "Sure. And that would be something that my ex would have done in a heartbeat." She looked up at Aiden and asked, "Did you get any new information?"

He shook his head. "No, but I requested a lot more intel." He faced the lawyer. "Have you been given any information about all six related murders to date?"

He shook his head. "Now we still have to sign paperwork to have her be represented by me."

Aiden raised an eyebrow and tilted his head. "And we may not even need those murder details. As soon as there's another one, she should be let off the hook."

"How do you figure?" the lawyer asked, looking at him.

Toby frowned at Aiden. "Do you really think that he'll

kill again?"

"He's certainly not slowed down at all," he noted, "and I think the cops are perfectly aware it's a ludicrous charge against you."

The lawyer nodded. "It is pretty ludicrous, but the cops must check every lead."

"Sure," Aiden agreed, with a negligent shrug. "But they're being lax, and I presume it's all about Moscow's father's influence."

The lawyer winced. "It is a little hard to get away from something like that in this town. There's definitely those with influence and those without."

"Well, I know where I fit in," Toby replied bitterly. "Nothing I told the cops ever made a difference. They never looked at anybody but me."

"It's fine," Aiden said. "We'll have this dealt with in no time."

She snorted. "I don't know what kind of magic elixir you're on, but I should get some for myself."

He smiled. "I get that," he admitted, "but honestly I'm not full of crap."

She shrugged and settled back.

The lawyer stood. "Hey, I've got to go. I have another appointment." He dropped a bunch of papers on the coffee table in front of her. "Go over these. If you want to work with me, then we'll set that in motion. However, you need to sign the attorney-client agreement first."

She nodded and watched as he left, then looked over at her cousin Mountain as he came back inside. "Is he your choice?"

"He's our choice," Mountain replied calmly. "You do need representation, unless it all goes away."

She added, "Aiden here seems to think he can pull enough threads to make it happen."

Mountain looked over at his friend. "You think so?"

"I'm pretty sure that we'll see another murder or two very quickly," he explained. "So we need to make sure that one of us sticks dead close to your cousin so that Toby has an alibi."

"All they'll do," she said, with renewed strength in her voice, "is look at you as being my accomplice."

He chuckled. "And yet I do have alibis for every other one of these murders."

She stared at him. "So you have a busy sex life or what?" She couldn't even believe she'd said that out loud. However, at the moment, if he had an alibi, he needed to prove it.

He looked over at Mountain, his lips twitching. "I was on a mission. And believe me. It's not something these local yokels or their bigwigs can argue away."

She collapsed against her chair. "Sorry. I didn't mean to get personal."

"Get personal," he assured her. "It's all good."

She stared at him. "I'm glad you're in a happy frame of mind."

"Why not?" Aiden said, with a shrug.

When the doorbell rang yet again, she groaned. "What is it with today?" she asked. "Dammit, I don't need all these interruptions."

Aiden stood and approached the front door.

"Who's at the door?" she asked.

He looked out and smiled. "The pizza is here."

"And you just left him standing there?"

"I wanted to wait until Mountain here stepped aside, so I could make sure I got to the pizza first and got a piece."

And, with that, he opened the front door.

She couldn't help but laugh. "He really does know you, doesn't he?" she said, with a smirk to Mountain.

"That's what you call a friend," he muttered, as he sniffed the air when the pizzas came wafting in. "I sure hope you ordered enough to fill me."

"Not enough pizza in the world for that," Aiden quipped, with a smile. He carried in three large boxes.

"So you figure three is enough to at least get Mountain somewhat full?" she teased. She sniffed the air and stated, "Maybe I'll have a piece too."

"No maybe about it," Aiden added cheerfully. "If you want to keep fighting the good fight, you have to keep up your energy, and that means food." He handed her a box.

"I don't need a whole pizza," she said. "Besides, I like my pizza on a plate."

"Have a plate. I don't mind." But Aiden had already opened the next box and pulled out a slice, which Mountain snagged right from Aiden's hands. With a mock look of outrage at his friend, Aiden snagged the next one, which appeared to be even bigger.

TOBY RETURNED WITH a plate, sat down, and pulled one piece each from two different kinds of pizzas, placing both on her plate.

The guys watched her and nodded.

"Good. Get that belly full first," Aiden noted. "So, that should be enough for you, right?"

In shock, she watched as the men devoured each piece in no time and realized that Aiden was seriously considering her ration of these pizzas. She immediately leaned forward and grabbed a third slice, just in case she had more of an appetite than she expected.

By the time she was full, after eating those first two slices, she was surprised that the bulk of the three pizzas were gone. She stared at the last few remaining pieces. "Good God, I forgot how much you eat," she said, staring at her cousin.

He gave her an offended look. "Hey, I wasn't alone in this pizza-eating contest, you know."

At that, she had to nod. "And he put away a ton of food too," she murmured, staring at Aiden.

Aiden shrugged. "I'm not as big as Mountain is, but I burn energy pretty fast. Now I need to go do some investigative legwork." He looked over at Mountain. "You'll stay here with her?"

"Nobody is staying here with me," she snapped in a hard tone.

"Then nobody is going anywhere," Aiden stated, sitting back down, "because you need an alibi for every step of the way from now on."

She stared at him blankly. "I don't even know what to say."

"Well, first off, let me go grab our bags from outside," Mountain suggested, and, with that, he disappeared.

Aiden stared at her, waiting for her response.

She was considering more objections. And, indeed, her mouth opened and closed a couple times, but the words just didn't seem to want to work.

He nodded. "It's one of the best decisions you've made yet."

Immediately her confused look turned into frustrated

anger.

"Don't even worry about getting angry," Aiden told her. "We're here to help. We'll help whether you like it or not."

"Good Lord," she exclaimed, "I thought Mountain was hard to deal with."

"Get used to it," Aiden stated. "You're my mission. Believe me. I have no intention of failing this op."

She stared at him in shock. "What, I'm some sort of test?"

"Absolutely not," he argued, "but, if you think I'll let anything happen to you, you're wrong."

She sank into her chair. "Do you think my life is in danger?" she whispered in horror.

"It never occurred to you, did it?"

"No." She frowned. "It still doesn't make any sense that it would be."

"Maybe not," he agreed, "but we can't take that chance. Right now someone is killing men connected to you, and a lot of hate is pointed in your direction."

She nodded. "Yeah, that message I got," she admitted. "I can't go to work even. Although, as I'm charged with murder, I can't imagine that'll be good for business."

"I can't imagine that it would be considered good for business either," he stated. "However, it's a curiosity factor."

She winced. "In that case, I'd rather not go to work, just to be gawked at and pointed at and talked about."

He chuckled. "Doesn't exactly make you feel better, does it?"

"No, not at all," she muttered. She stared at him. "I don't understand why you're so happy-go-lucky."

"What's not to like?" he asked. "Everything is good in my world."

"Sure," she groaned. "Your world isn't my world." Immediately Aiden's smile fell away, and she watched as he switched to wearing a concerned look on his face.

"And you're right there," he confirmed. "I'm not trying to make light of it, but I do know about these kinds of things, and that the sooner we can nip them in the bud, the better."

"And you've got a magical formula to get the cops to back off?"

"Well, like I told you earlier, your alibi for the next murder."

"Which murder may never happen, and how horrible to know another person has to die before I'm off the hook," she muttered. She picked up her third slice of pizza and slowly worked away on it.

"Any chance of a coffee?" he asked, "or do I have to order that in?"

She nodded toward the kitchen. "Help yourself."

He jumped to his feet and headed into the kitchen as if it were the most natural thing in the world. When Mountain returned with their bags, he headed upstairs and dropped them off in the nearest spare bedroom and then came back down, bringing his bedroll to the living room.

"There's another spare bedroom upstairs," Toby said. "You know that."

"I do know that," he agreed, "but one of us should be upstairs, and one should be downstairs. And I elect Aiden to be upstairs."

She stared at him. "Why?" she muttered.

"Because he cares. He's all heart, and you and I are still walking around each other like we're on tenterhooks."

"Yeah," she noted, "it's been a couple rough years."

"And I wasn't there when I should have been."

"And I wasn't there for you either," she admitted, "when your family went through shit."

"Still going through shit," he stated in a quiet tone. "You have no idea." At that, she stopped and looked at him. He held up a hand and shook his head. "No, I'm not talking until we get your stuff dealt with."

"Yeah, and when would that be?"

"I'll give Aiden maybe forty-eight hours," he replied, looking at his watch, "because I don't have much more time than that."

"Good God, what are you talking about?"

"I'm waiting on information. As soon as that intel comes in, I'll have to book it."

She nodded, almost numb. "Okay. And where will you go?"

He stared at her for a long moment. "It's better if you don't know yet."

She shook her head. "You know that doesn't work for me."

Just then, Aiden stepped into the living room. "Coffee is on." Aiden stared at his buddy and frowned. "*Uh-oh,* ... heavy talk again."

She groaned. "Is there ever anything other than heavy talk with us?"

"Sure there is," Aiden countered, "just not necessarily the kind of talk you want to have."

"Absolutely *not* the kind of talk I want to have," she whispered. She turned to her cousin. "Later."

"Sure," he agreed, "later."

ANOTHER BUZZ CAME from Aiden's phone. As the requested info kept coming in, his phone was slowing way down. He looked over at Mountain. "Did you bring in my laptop?"

Mountain nodded. "Upstairs on your bed."

At that, Aiden bolted upstairs, snatched his laptop, and came down again with the charger in hand. "We've got a lot of incoming files," he explained. "It'll be easier to go through some of them on the computer."

# CHAPTER 4

"WHAT FILES?" TOBY asked curiously, walking over and handing Aiden a cup of coffee.

"Thank you," he murmured, as he looked up at her with a bright smile.

She flushed and sat down again. "It's the least I can do," she noted, with a shrug.

He nodded. "Otherwise Mountain might get upset at your lack of hospitality."

She rolled her eyes at that. "The day that Mountain got to dictate anything in my world was a long time ago," she muttered.

"Still don't quite know what happened between you two."

"Just family stuff," she replied, "and stuff that, in a way, we've already kind of worked through."

"Good," Aiden said. He moved to the coffee table and plugged in his laptop.

"You haven't told me what files."

"I have all the police files on the murders," he told her. "The only way we'll really get you off the hook permanently—so it's not a stain on your public record—is to solve this."

She sat down hard. "How did you get the police files?"

He looked at her innocently and replied, "Legit avenues.

I asked for it, and I got it."

"Sure," she quipped, with another eye roll.

"Well, it's true. Don't believe me if you don't want to. That's fine," he noted. "We haven't done anything wrong."

"Says you," she added.

Mountain sat down beside Aiden. "I've got my laptop too," Mountain said. "Shoot me copies." And, with that, the two men buried themselves in reading those files. "Really not a whole lot here," Mountain said after a while. "As far as the cops are concerned, the connection to Toby is the fact that they were at your table."

"Sure." She groaned. "However, do you have any idea how many hundreds, if not thousands, of people go through my table on a weekly basis?"

Both Mountain and Aiden nodded. "I can imagine, particularly if ..." Aiden stopped and snorted. "Okay. So this is partly why your table so popular."

She winced, knowing what was coming.

He looked up, studied her face, and nodded. "Somebody decided you were his lucky charm."

"That's just what that one customer called me," she argued, wincing. "Definitely not my terminology."

"No," Aiden admitted, "but that meant everybody in the casino wanted to come to your table."

"And that doesn't make any of the other dealers very happy either," she noted. "So it causes added trouble at work too."

"Which just brings up more suspects."

"Nobody will kill these winners because they're jealous that I have more people at my table," she declared, staring at him in shock.

"People do all kinds of shit for all kinds of shitty reasons," he shared. "Would I think that would happen? No, but that doesn't mean I'm not wrong."

Mountain nodded at that. "And you've got a point. The fact that this was publicized and that your nickname was utilized, that would bring an awful lot of people to you, even if you didn't know who they were."

"In casinos, there are always a lot of onlookers. And that's to be expected to a certain degree because, once people are winning, everybody wants to hang around. It's like the gold dust might rub off on them." Such a cynical note filled her tone that she winced. "Hey, look. I'm sorry. I'm not trying to be a downer about this. Generally I enjoy my job."

"And you're good at it," Mountain stated.

She nodded. "I'm good at it."

"You don't gamble?" Aiden asked.

"I'm not allowed to gamble." At that, both men stopped and looked at her. She groaned. "I'm sure that's another motive that they'll tell you about whenever we talk about trying to clear my name."

"And what's that?" Aiden asked.

"The casino—where I now work—thought I was card counting one time," she admitted.

"Were you card counting?" Mountain asked.

She gave her cousin a flat stare but didn't say anything.

"You were?" Mountain huffed. "And here I told Aiden that you were brilliant."

She shrugged. "Math for me is dead easy. I mean, it's not even that I was necessarily card counting, but how are you *not* supposed to count cards when you can see them flying in your mind?"

"Right," Mountain grumbled. "So, for you, the cards are a problem."

"Exactly. Hey, once that skill is turned on, it doesn't shut off. So I got hauled into the manager's office, and, when they realized who I was, it was a case of never darken their door again because, as far as they were concerned, I was a cheater. Yet they offered me a job as a dealer, explaining that I should work for them and find other cheaters."

"And you went along with that?" Aiden asked.

"Well, if I couldn't play poker," she explained, "I needed gainful employment, and I didn't really want to be banned from all the casinos."

"Do you still go?"

"Every once in a while," she admitted, "when I need a little cash."

"And that's all you win?"

"Sure." She nodded. "Anything other than that gets me into trouble. Doesn't matter if it's legit or not. I don't get the opportunity of having somebody look at me and think it's legit. I'm automatically considered a thief."

"Interesting," Aiden noted.

"Goes along with the territory." Toby shrugged.

"And how did your father handle you being picked up for card counting?" Aiden asked.

She gave him another flat stare. "See? That's another thing you know that would never be allowed in my world or in his. I'm sure somebody contacted him and told him, but, once I had the dealer job working at the casino, it seemed like my father didn't quite know what to do with that and wasn't sure if he should believe in the cheating rumors or not."

"Did he ever ask you?" Aiden asked her.

She shook her head immediately. "No. Would I have lied to him? No. But I'm glad I didn't have to get into that conversation because my parents wouldn't have believed me anyway."

"Nice family," Aiden quipped.

"*Not*," she replied. "The only good part of my family is Mountain." At that, she looked over at Mountain and added, "It's just that, when he's in trouble and needs help, he's not very good at asking for help."

He looked up at her pointedly and said, "Yeah? And how good are you at asking for help?"

She flushed at that. "Well, you're here now, so hopefully I'm getting better at it."

He shook his head. "You still suck at asking for help."

"Well, I can't say that you're getting any better at it yourself."

"No, I'm sure not," he admitted, "but, most of the time, I'm out there helping other people and don't need assistance myself."

"But everybody needs help some of the time," Toby noted.

He gave her a warm smile. "So true."

She flushed yet again, now realizing that, as far as he was concerned, they were talking about her. In a few minutes, she looked over at Aiden, who was involved in the files. "Anything interesting?"

"Lots interesting," he replied, "absolutely nothing that ties this to you."

"You mean, outside of the fact that these dead gamblers were at my table at some point?"

"Your table, yes, and that you have no alibi, but that'll go for a tremendous amount of other people in this city."

"Well, not those at the tables," she noted. "A lot of dealers and dozens of other casino workers are on shift at any given time."

"So, if they wanted to," Aiden said, "the police could pull the video cameras, and they could double-check where these people were at other people's tables at the same time, correct?"

She shrugged. "Good luck getting the video cameras."

At that, Aiden brought up a Chat box on his laptop and typed away.

She looked over at Mountain and frowned.

Mountain shrugged. "We have access to stuff."

"Says you," she scoffed. "Access to good stuff or is it illegal access to stuff?"

"Not against the law," Mountain declared. "Anything that the cops have, we're entitled to."

She shook her head. "You know I don't really think that's true."

"Don't worry about it," he said. "We'd never do anything to jeopardize your case."

She frowned. "Maybe not, but I'm not sure that other people won't."

He stood at her side and studied her face for a moment. "I'm not sure what that means."

"I just feel like other people, potentially Moscow's father, are manipulating all this," she suggested.

"Absolutely he is, and there's a good chance that the cops are trying to make you fit their murder pattern," he stated. "But, once we have video feeds to debunk everything they say about you," he explained, "then there won't be a legal leg to stand on."

"And what about an illegal leg?" she asked.

Mountain nodded. "We always have to consider that. How much does Moscow's father hate you?"

"You have no idea," she replied.

"Then he's somebody we'll look into further."

At that, Aiden raised his head and confirmed, "I've already asked for a full rundown on your father-in-law."

"Don't call him that," she snapped. He stared at her, and she immediately shook her head. "Sorry, but that's definitely a touchy subject with me."

"But you did legally marry Moscow, right?"

"Yes," she admitted. "And thankfully I don't have to go through the process of divorcing him."

"No, you sure don't," Aiden noted, "and, of course, that is more motive."

She glared at him. "I didn't kill him."

"I know," he agreed, "but the cops don't know that yet."

"And why don't they?" she asked. "I can't believe that this has gone on as long as it has."

"Because they're still trying to look for something to nail you with," Mountain explained. "Just relax. We will get there."

She nodded slowly. "If you don't mind, I'm going upstairs to lie down. It's been a very nerve-racking day."

"Did the lawyer say anything else to you?"

She pointed at the paperwork on the coffee table. "Read and sign the paperwork, lots and lots of paperwork," she said bitterly. "Like I haven't seen enough paperwork in a very long time."

"That's all right to deal with later," Aiden replied. "I'll be up in a little bit." She looked at him nonplussed. He smiled. "Where you are, I will be."

She shook her head at that. "It's a waste of time. It'd be way too obvious for somebody else to get killed now, and it still won't stop the case against me for supposedly murdering my ex."

"You always call him your ex."

"Always," she snapped. "It's more than I can stomach to remember that I married him, and I know it'll sound even worse, but thank God he's gone. Thank God I don't have to deal with the repercussions of having him around on a daily basis." And, with that, she stormed up the stairs.

⚓

AIDEN LOOKED OVER at Mountain. "I don't like the inference that the cops are not being honest."

"In a town like this?" Mountain raised one eyebrow. "And remember. I grew up here. It's all about who you know."

"It should be about the law."

Mountain shrugged. "It will be the end result, but, if they can make it fit, they will."

"Surely the DA will be on top of whether the evidence will be something that'll make a case or not."

"Also depends if the DA is in the father-in-law's pocket."

Just then came a *ding*. Aiden looked down at his phone. "Well, that's good timing. Father-in-law's file just arrived."

"Good," Mountain said, "let me take a look." Aiden sent him the file, and Mountain nodded. "Now that we have all this, should be absolutely no way to not get this sorted."

"Yeah, that just means what we really need is," Aiden stated, "proof that she's in the clear, which, of course, she isn't yet."

"No," Mountain replied. "The information through the Mavericks seems to flow pretty well."

"It does." Aiden looked over at his buddy. "Is that part

of what you're testing?"

"Partly," he noted. "Let's just say that I've got a really nasty suspicion that I'll need a hell of a lot of help to fix this other problem of mine."

"And yet you're still not ready to talk?"

"No, not yet," he confirmed. "Last thing I want to do is put you in jeopardy."

At that, Aiden looked over at his friend and raised an eyebrow. "That bad?"

"Hell, yes," he snapped. "That bad."

"Okay. Well, we each need to get through this, and we'll talk soon about your other op."

"Yeah. Well, I don't have a whole lot of time," Mountain explained. "So, if I don't get this finished with you, I may have to leave you alone to handle this."

At that, Aiden stared at him. "I'm not sure exactly what that means," he admitted, "but obviously this other op of yours is urgent."

"I keep trying to contact somebody, and I had communication two days ago," he shared. "Then bad weather set in, and I'm not sure whether that's part of the problem now or whether we're heading in a direction I don't want to go."

Aiden couldn't really make a whole lot of sense from that, but, as Mountain got up and started pacing, Aiden realized Mountain would only tell Aiden so much. "When you're ready to talk, let me know," he said gently.

Mountain immediately nodded. "Will do."

With that, Aiden had to be satisfied. He started poring over Daddy's file. "This guy owns a casino," he said.

"Yeah, one of the smaller ones."

"But he owns it outright apparently. Have you had any dealings with him before?"

Mountain shook his head immediately. "No. But don't forget I'm the black sheep of the family."

"So is Toby apparently," Aiden noted in a noncommittal voice.

"That's true," he murmured.

Aiden added, "And her daddy? I don't think he will do anything to help, which to me is just mind-boggling."

"That's because you're a romantic, and you want things to work out well for everyone," Mountain stated.

Aiden stared at his buddy in shock. "A romantic?" He almost felt insulted.

Mountain quirked his lips at him. "Yeah, a romantic. You'd like nothing better than to go upstairs and to tell Toby that this will all go away."

"Of course I would like to do that," Aiden agreed, "but I'm not naïve, and I certainly know it won't go away just because I want it to."

"I hear you," Mountain noted. "And sometimes the shit just doesn't stop falling."

Again Aiden figured it came back to something else in Mountain's life. Aiden frowned. "I like her," he announced.

Mountain smiled. "I know, and honestly the two of you look good together."

That was another eye-opener for Aiden. "Which has absolutely nothing to do with what we're here about," he stated immediately.

"Hey, you now know that I'm not against the two of you hooking up. It's just that she's in a delicate position at present."

"I'm not looking at hooking up with anybody," Aiden stated in a dry tone, "and never on the job."

"I don't know. According to some of the things that I

understand are going on in the Mavericks," Mountain stated, "that's not necessarily been true for everyone."

Aiden shrugged. "Yeah. I heard. I still have that weird code."

"That code will get you killed," Mountain replied absentmindedly.

"I hope not," Aiden countered. "It's the one that I live by."

"And that's not done you a whole lot of good, has it?"

"Neither has it hurt." Aiden looked at his friend, worried. "You've really got some bee in your bonnet right now."

Mountain slumped into the chair beside him. "I do," he admitted. "Sorry. I'm not trying to bitch my way out of here."

"Let's focus and get your cousin out of trouble," Aiden said, "then we can go deal with your problem."

He looked over at Aiden and smiled. "That wouldn't be a bad idea. I want to have a talk with the father-in-law."

"Is that smart?" Aiden asked.

"Hell no, it's not smart," Mountain agreed, "but I also want to check the crime scene locations."

At that, they looked up to see Toby coming down the stairs, her arms wrapped around her chest. She glared at her cousin. "I heard all of that, and I can't sleep now," she announced.

"In that case, maybe you should come with us," Aiden suggested, making a decision. "We'll go check out the crime scenes."

"It's not a good idea to take her with us," Mountain argued.

"And it's not a good idea to leave me behind," she argued in a smug tone. "So, the only option is to take me with you."

Mountain obviously didn't like it, but Aiden nodded. "Grab a sweater." She looked at him, and he shrugged. "It's cloudy out and kind of misty."

"It's still Vegas," she declared.

"Fine," he said. "But maybe put up your hair so that that long hair isn't quite so discernible."

"Are we going in disguise?"

"Not necessarily," Aiden shared, "but I definitely want to make sure that you aren't easily picked off as being highly visible." She obviously didn't know what he meant by that. "I just don't want everybody to be pointing fingers at you."

"Oh, great," she muttered in disgust. "I hadn't considered that."

"No, and you need to," he murmured. "Things could get dicey."

"Not *could*," Mountain murmured, "*will*." He looked over at his cousin. "Put it up under a baseball cap. Your profile is pretty distinctive anyway, so we won't have a whole lot of luck in trying to disguise you that easily," he explained. "We just want it to be a first-glance rejection kind of thing."

She nodded, walked over to the front closet, pulled out a baseball cap, tossed it on her head, and asked, "How about this?"

"That'll work," Mountain noted, "particularly if you take that hair and put it up."

She groaned and removed the cap. Then she immediately screwed her hair up into a bun, grabbed a clip off the side table, where she'd tossed it after coming home from work, and put the hat on again. At that, they all trooped outside again.

Aiden looked at her and added, "Unless you'd really rather stay home."

"Doesn't matter what I'd rather do," she replied calmly. "If you guys are out here trying to help, the least I can do is try and help too."

"Unless there's nothing you can do," he noted.

"According to Mountain, there is."

"And, if nothing else," Aiden said, "you and your cousin are in agreement over that."

She shrugged. "I'd be a fool to not believe him. I know he has an awful lot of skills that I don't know about."

"And you trust him?"

"Yes, absolutely." Toby looked over at Aiden. "I absolutely trust him."

"Good," Aiden said. "Then you need to put me in the same category of trust, and, if I tell you to do something, whether at home or in the field, you must do it without question," he declared, his voice turning hard.

She glared at him. "Doesn't mean I'll listen to you."

"Then you're not leaving this house," he snapped. "My way or the highway." She stared at him open-mouthed. He shrugged. "Make a decision, or else I'm staying here, and Mountain is going alone."

She didn't like hearing any of that. She looked over a Mountain. He just stared back at her. She asked her cousin, "And you agree to this?"

"Aiden is a good guy. And very few men are out there I'd trust with your life," Mountain said, "but he's one of them."

She threw up her hands in disgust. "Fine. Go all macho, then see if I care."

At that, Mountain snickered. "Hey, it could be way worse. We could not give a damn. Then where would you be?"

# CHAPTER 5

TOBY GAVE AIDEN a quick tour of the city, as Mountain drove. "That's the casino where I work." She pointed to the big fountain splashing outside. He nodded, and Mountain kept on driving. "You don't care about that one?" she asked the guys.

"No, I want to see the crime scenes." And, one by one, checking each crime-scene location noted in the police's case files, they went from place to place, the street numbers and addresses already input into Aiden's phone.

When Mountain stopped at one, she fell silent.

"I guess this is the one then, isn't it?" Aiden asked her.

She frowned. "The one what?"

"The one where your husband was killed."

She nodded slowly. "Although I've told you that I don't like that word."

"It's legally correct," Aiden noted, "so don't get upset when people use it without thinking."

She didn't say anything because he was right. Just because she was against the word didn't mean that it would stop the word from being used.

Aiden got out with Mountain at his side, who took several photos. Aiden marked it on a map and then walked around. "Do you know who found him?"

She shrugged. "I don't have any information on that."

"We can find out," Aiden noted, as he looked through the files. "It just says a passerby." As he looked around, he shook his head. "It's hardly a passerby area."

"Probably a druggie," she guessed. "This is a popular area for drug deals."

"Did your husband use drugs?"

"No." And then she stopped. "Honestly I don't know anything about him really."

It was such an odd comment to make that Aiden looked over at her in surprise.

She shrugged. "And we're back to that again. I really don't know anything, except that he's a bully and made my and Michelle's life miserable."

"Got it," Aiden replied. And, with that, they continued on to the next address and then the next.

By the time they were done at the last crime scene, she asked, "And what exactly did any of that tell you?"

Aiden faced her and explained, "They all center within the same six blocks. They're all close enough to the strip that it could have been any number of reasons to use these Dumpsters at these locations."

"But mostly because these guys were robbed and murdered," she noted.

"Right," Aiden agreed. "So, it makes sense that they would come out of the casino—high on whatever drug of their choice, including just gambling—and may have had a friend in common or may have had, you know, a cab in common or something with the victims. ... I need to do an in-depth look into each of the characters."

"I already did a bunch," Mountain relayed. "Two of them were visitors on holiday. One of them was a local man, and one of them was a regular but an upstanding citizen supposedly," he said, with more of a mocking tone than anything.

"And what about Moscow?" Aiden asked Mountain.

"He was a gambler with a gambling problem," he stated. "Honestly you can't trust that type at any time."

At that, she nodded. "And I would agree with that. Moscow and I both come from gambling families. We know how devastating it can be."

"And yet you went gambling yourself," Aiden told her.

"I went gambling because I needed the money," she said, "and I'm good at it. The fact is, the casinos don't really want me to be around, so I had to find another way. I got tired of the confrontations. I would walk in, and they would basically tell me that I wasn't welcome."

"Got it," Aiden noted. "Do you think that was about you and your card-counting abilities, or was that about your dad owning his own casino or some other influence, like Moscow's father?"

"I have no idea," she replied, frowning at Aiden. "I assumed it was just about me."

"And yet I'm not so sure that that would be a fair assessment," Mountain stated.

"Regardless," Aiden replied, facing Toby, "I'll give you the names and pictures of the gamblers who died and see if you know them."

"The cops already did that," she said. "I knew them only from visiting my table."

"So, you had no social life with them at all?" Aiden asked her.

"I had no social life," she declared, with a bitterness that was hard to ignore. "Remember my ex?"

Aiden nodded. "Right. Got that. And so none of these

dead men are memorable in any way."

"Not particularly," she said. "I mean, obviously there might have been something that made them memorable but to me? Not necessarily."

"And how often do you get big winners?"

"Often enough that it becomes commonplace," she replied.

Aiden added, "And by *big*, I mean the whales playing at a completely different table."

"I wasn't dealing with the whales."

"Meaning, the big spenders?" Aiden asked to confirm.

"Sure. They get a lot of special treatment, and they get an awful lot of extras and freebies," she noted. "They don't necessarily come to somebody like me."

"And yet if you had that lucky name?" Mountain asked.

"And I did." She winced. "I was asked to work a couple tables for private parties, but it's not my favorite gig."

"Why is that?" Aiden asked.

"Because of the booze and the groping hands," she replied, with a roll of her eyes. "This is all about money, and, in that case, those men don't stick out to me."

"And you didn't see them any more than you would expect to see any of the other gamblers?"

"No, not at all." She looked at the photo of the last dead guy, frowned, and added, "He did ask me on the last night that I worked if I liked working there, but that was such a nondescript kind of question. I mean, it's not as if I ever think about it. It's a job. I do it because it's what I do to pay my bills."

At that, Aiden nodded. "And that's quite true, isn't it?"

"Sure. I mean, you do what you have to do." She frowned. "The other two out-of-towners I don't even remember. Which sounds terrible because they had families and somebody should remember them," she murmured, as she studied their faces on his phone. She swiped through the pictures one more time, shrugged, and returned Aiden's phone to him. "Honestly? Not a whole lot is memorable about any of them."

At that, Mountain added, "They were all stabbed too."

"Which is upfront and personal," she noted, "and definitely not something I would choose." She gave a light shudder.

"Why in particular?"

"Well, for me," she explained, "I don't have any martial arts skills or very much in the way of self-defense skills, so to kill a man that way would be very hard. I mean, I couldn't subdue him."

"We already know that it's not you," Aiden replied, "so what we need is more proof that we can turn the cops in the right direction."

"In that case," she snapped, "you need to get my ex's father off their backs."

"And we'll try that too," Aiden confirmed, with a look over at Mountain.

Mountain nodded. "And the thing is, he has also got lots of security. So it's not as if we just walk in and tell him to smarten up."

"Right," Aiden agreed. "And you guys know him."

"Know *of* him," Mountain corrected. "I've never had any direct dealings with him." He looked over at his cousin. "You?"

She shook her head. "No. And you know Dad always told us to stay away from them."

"Why is that?" Aiden asked them.

"Because he's bad news," Mountain said. "But you know? There's an awful lot of talk about gangs, drugs, and money laundering through the casinos, etcetera. Toby's father would say that none of that ever happens, but I'm not so sure, and he would certainly be looking to keep his own job, which pays very well."

She snorted at that. "As you well know, it's about the only thing that matters to my parents."

"What about the big fancy house?" Mountain asked.

"That would be the other thing that matters to my parents. And it is high-end, worth millions," she noted, "but it won't help me any. They don't share. Remember?" At that, Aiden looked at her in surprise. She shrugged. "My dad was always of the opinion that, if you wanted anything in life, you needed to work for it yourself."

"Well, I get that," Aiden agreed, "but being charged for murder hardly compares to something you can easily handle on your own."

"He would say that I got into hot water all on my own. Then I can get out of it on my own." She looked over at Mountain. "Wouldn't he?"

Mountain nodded. "Yeah. That's definitely the way he looks at life."

Toby asked him, "So, why did you try to make it look like he was the one paying the attorney's bill for this?"

He sighed. "Because I didn't think you would allow me to help."

"I'm not a fool."

"Yeah, that's true," he noted. "How did you know?"

"I repeat. I'm also not a fool." She raised her eyebrow at him.

He smiled. "Nope, that you definitely aren't." He looked

back over at Aiden. "Her father won't be easy."

"Even though you're family?"

"Definitely being family, we'll be told to butt out and to let the law do their job."

"Even when the law isn't working?"

"He'll say that she got herself into trouble and that she needs to get herself out of it."

"Wow. I hate him already," Aiden muttered. At her frown, he shrugged. "Not everybody has to be an asshole. Some of them just choose to be."

She snickered at that. "That's my family. It's all about how well they can make a living off of Vegas before they retire."

"And do you expect them to retire?"

"One day," she said, "at least maybe. I really don't know whether they'll manage it or not."

"Which is an interesting comment," Aiden noted. "Do you really see them as staying here for the rest of their lives?"

"I don't know," she murmured. "My father said that he would never stay in Vegas forever, but you know that—with that kind of paycheck, with that kind of notoriety, with that kind of influence—it's hard to walk away from."

Aiden nodded. "I can see that, but it's also a little disconcerting if we don't really believe that he'll be there to help. The next question is, Will he be there to hurt?"

"Maybe," she said calmly. "And I think if my lovely *father-in-law*," she added, sending him a mocking look at the term, "were to push dear old Dad's buttons, he might very well buckle."

"And again very interesting," Aiden noted, with a frown.

"They're all shits," Mountain confirmed, "but we don't get to pick and choose our family. We get to pick and choose what we do in terms of a relationship with them, but that's it."

"And your relationship is?" Aiden asked his buddy.

"They're shits," he repeated cheerfully. "The only one worth anything is her," he said, with a nod to Toby.

She smiled. "I'm glad you said that," she added in a rueful tone.

"Sometimes I wonder if that's even fair. You're not your father. You're not your mother," he reminded her.

"I know," she agreed, "but it's kind of hard growing up with that kind of attitude from them."

"And did I hear you say you had a sister?" Aiden asked her.

She nodded slowly. "Yes, I do."

"And?"

"And what?" she replied. "She's married to a gambler."

"Oh." Aiden stared at her for a long moment.

"Yep, but they don't live here. And that's a good thing. He made big money, and he took off with her."

"Also interesting. And how did your family handle that?"

"They were pissed. What do you expect? She wasn't supposed to marry a gambler—that's just a downward path of no return, as far as my dad is concerned."

"Right. And, of course, he knows best."

"He'd like to think so," she replied, with a bright smile.

"Do you have any contact with her?"

"Nope, not at all," she said. "And I highly suspect that I won't for the rest of my life either."

AIDEN DIDN'T EVEN know what to think about that, as they

arrived home once more. That was so foreign to him and to his concept of family life; it was just a very strange scenario. Mountain never talked about his family, and the fact that this was his extended family just made it that much more interesting to Aiden. "Okay, in that case, I guess there's no point in interviewing your dad."

"Nope. And he wouldn't thank you for it either. And, if you walk into his casino and try to grill him, you'll get your butt kicked out on the street."

He looked over at Mountain.

Mountain nodded. "Believe her."

"Well, we're not getting anywhere fast then," Aiden replied in frustration.

She shrugged. "Yeah, we know that, but you also just got here."

He stared at her. "I don't care if I just got here or not. As far as I'm concerned, I should already have something. And yet I'm still tracking down leads."

She shook her head. "Whatever. I'm heading up to bed." And, with that, she turned and climbed the stairs.

He watched her leave and then faced Mountain.

"I'll crash too." Mountain added, "You're on first watch."

He nodded. "Are we really expecting some danger to her? Seems she's the fall guy in all this mess."

"No, not at all," Mountain said. "But, if you'll be up anyway, keep an eye on her."

"Will do," he murmured.

And, with that, Mountain walked over to the long couch, stretched out, and closed his eyes.

Really, it wasn't a bad idea to keep watch. Aiden was still kind of wired from all the information floating in his brain and so would be up for hours anyway. What they had really was a couple different scenarios, most of which didn't even involve Toby. Her husband was murdered, but so were now five other men, all in similar circumstances, and one nasty-ass father-in-law was trying to make Toby's life difficult. Yet no evidence implicated her as the murderer of her husband, much less all six guys. And that was the thing.

How dare the cops charge her when they couldn't make a case? But, of course, they could drop the charges at any time. However, it's still messing up her life. Was that their plan? It was working. Aiden sent Corbin a text, asking for any forensic information on the murder files because, as far as he saw from the information he had been sent, there wasn't any.

Corbin phoned him. "It's still in forensics."

"Of course. That's why nothing is in the file. Finger-prints? Tox-screens?"

"Same thing," Corbin stated. "Nothing is back. Nothing is conclusive. Nothing ties her to these murders," he said.

"Just motive."

"But, if that's all there is, there's an awful lot of motive for other people to kill all these men too. They were all carrying a substantial amount of cash, confirmed in just hours for some, before their bodies were found."

"Even her husband?" Aiden frowned at that and checked the file.

"Inconclusive," Corbin stated.

Since she'd already gone up to bed, Aiden couldn't ask her, and would she even know?

"According to the police, he was in the casino that evening," Corbin read from the file.

"But everybody here in Vegas is in the casinos in the

evenings," he replied. "That's like the local pastime, basically the whole purpose for Vegas."

"For the diehards, yes, but not necessarily for the working folk in Vegas, who just are trying to pay their bills and keep a roof over their head. Now Moscow? He was a gambler. His father was a casino owner, so Moscow was raised in that environment. I don't see that he'll be very much different from other addicted gamblers."

"Maybe the murderer didn't get as much money from Moscow?" Aiden mused out loud, "but chances are that he was still carrying a substantial amount."

"That's likely."

"And why would he want to carry that kind of cash?" Aiden muttered. But, of course, that just made it easier and faster to cash out—not like when requesting a cashier's check. So, if you wanted actual cash, that led to less red tape and time, which also kept a lot of things quiet and under the table, so his gambling life just kept on going.

At that thought, Aiden asked Corbin for the street cameras on the casino strip to see what he could find on the night that her husband died. When Aiden got a copy of that, he headed to his laptop and brought up the feed. He watched as Moscow stepped out of the casino and headed down the strip.

Multiple cameras later, Aiden picked up Moscow, going down several more blocks. And then he jerked his head to the right, and a smile broke out across his face, and he disappeared from sight. Aiden checked the location and noted it was the alley where he was killed. Someone had called out to him. Someone who obviously knew Moscow. That wouldn't necessarily help Toby's argument either because she would have been somebody that Moscow would have immediately gone to.

Which was also a very strange scenario. Their whole relationship and subsequent marriage was strange. But the fact that Moscow had agreed to Toby's marriage rules said a lot about the strange setup. Yet Aiden was certain, had Moscow lived, he never would have abided by Toby's rules. From what Aiden knew of Moscow so far, that man had his own plans to set into motion.

Aiden looked down at his phone. "I need Moscow's address." And when he found that in the police report, Aiden looked over at Mountain, who was lying there, wide awake. "You okay if I go take a look at her ex's apartment?"

"Yeah. You want me to come?"

"We can't," Aiden said. "We can't leave her unprotected, without an alibi."

Mountain frowned at that and nodded. "If you see anything, you call me."

"Will do," Aiden replied.

# CHAPTER 6

TOBY HEARD A door open and then murmured voices. She immediately got up, went down to the living room, and only found Mountain. "Hey. What's going on?"

"Aiden's going over to Moscow's place," Mountain told her. "Aiden tracked Moscow on the street cams, all the way from your casino to the alleyway, where the cops found Moscow's blood," telling her what they'd seen on Moscow's clip.

She frowned. "Which just makes it sound like it's me."

"And yet why would you be in the alleyway?"

"Well, according to the cops," she quipped, "to kill him obviously."

He smiled gently. "And yet you didn't, and we know that."

"Well, I'm glad you do," she said on a sigh, "because I'm not sure that very many other people will."

"Anyway, we also have the fact that several other people were killed in alleyways," he added, "so not to worry."

"And what about me? We all could have gone to Moscow's apartment together."

He looked at her. "Do you have keys?"

She shrugged. "He keeps one outside on the porch."

"Whereabouts?" he asked. "I'll text it to Aiden."

She gave him the location, and he quickly fired off a

91

text, while she waited. "I'd rather have gone."

"Well, if we need to go back, we all will," Mountain noted. "Right now, he just wanted to get a general lay of the land."

"Yet Moscow wasn't killed there."

"Doesn't mean anything. If Moscow was involved in any strange deals or something wonky was going on, Aiden'll find it."

"Maybe," she murmured. "Doesn't mean it'll do me a damn bit of good though."

He frowned at her. "Hey, stay strong."

"I am," she snapped. "Seems like all I've ever been."

"No, and you're right," he agreed. "I'm sorry. I should have been there for you when Moscow started to get really abusive."

She shrugged. "You were dealing with your own problems. We just basically expected the other to be there, and we couldn't. It's not a big deal, and I am really happy to see you now."

He grinned. "Me too, seems like a long time."

"Too long," she muttered. She then groaned, closed her eyes, and asked, "How long will Aiden be out there?"

"Not long," Moscow guessed, "maybe an hour."

She plunked herself on a nearby chair and said, "So, tell me about him."

"What do you want to know?" he asked, but she felt the interest in his gaze.

She flushed, then closed her eyes. "He's interesting."

"Oh, that kind of interesting, huh?"

She opened her eyes and glared at her cousin.

Mountain nodded. "Aiden's honest, honorable, and he'd never lie, cheat, or steal. He has fought for his country more than most people would ever find out about," he added. "And I trust him—I trust him with my back, your back, and anybody in my team. I'm not sure what else I can tell you."

She studied him for a long moment. "That says an awful lot."

"It does. He's a good guy," Mountain declared. "I wouldn't be at all upset if the two of you hooked up."

"Well, I don't know about that," she said. "He's very focused on his job."

"And yet he expected to already have made some progress by now," Mountain noted, with a wry look.

"And you?"

"Anything in Vegas becomes very twisted, once you factor in the money and the power angles. It all corrupts," Mountain stated. "So, we'll do the best we can, as fast as we can, but I don't guarantee that the time frame here will ever be anything that is workable."

"It never is, is it?" she said, rolling her neck.

"You okay?"

"Yeah, I'm okay," she murmured. "It just sucks."

"And that it does," he agreed, with a nod. "But that doesn't mean that it'll always suck," he added. "Right now, things are tough. But we will get to the bottom of this."

"Now that I have you in my corner, yeah," she admitted. "When I got up this morning, I wasn't sure that it was even worth getting out of bed. The cops have been on my case for a long time, driving me crazy, especially over the last couple weeks, and it doesn't seem fair."

"Nope. But a long time really isn't a long time when it comes to this kind of stuff. Moscow has only been dead for two weeks."

She nodded. "Yeah, *two weeks*. It seems like a lifetime."

"But it should be a good life now. He made your life a living hell."

She nodded. Just then her phone rang. She looked down at it winced.

"What is it?"

"It's Michelle, Moscow's sister." She answered it. "Michelle, what's wrong?" The sounds of her crying on the other end could be heard by her and Mountain as well. Toby slumped a little bit deeper into her chair. "I'm sorry you're having bad dreams," she said. "Remember. He's dead. I promise you that he's dead. … Yes, I know it for sure. He's not coming back to harm you." She pinched the bridge of her nose, wishing she had some way to get through to Michelle that her brother was dead and gone and could no longer hurt her.

Only after she finally calmed down Michelle and got off the phone did she note how intently Mountain stared at her.

"Hey"—she shrugged—"that's the kind of stuff that Michelle's been doing for a very long time."

"Moscow really was a bastard to her, wasn't he?"

She nodded. "To both of us," she said, rubbing her arms.

"Did he beat you up more than the one time?"

She gave him a ghost of a smile. "When you're the one getting beaten, it seems like it's forever, and then you try to justify it, or you try to find a way to explain it or to even forget it," she explained. "In my case, I never could. There was just no justification for what he did, and I was terrified of him before that even happened. All the beating did was reinforce the idea that I needed to get the hell away from him."

"And yet when he applied pressure, you buckled."

She gave him a sad look. "You don't deal with Michelle on a regular basis. And there's just no helping her sometimes," she murmured. "Even though I tried so very hard for so long, sometimes you just can't get through to her."

"I'm sorry to know that you took that kind of beating because of his sister."

"And Moscow knew it and knew that I would do anything to try and protect Michelle. And even now that she's safe, it's not the same thing for her. She's still caught in this loop of terror."

He nodded slowly. "I'm so sorry for that. And you have the patience of a saint."

She shook her head. "I don't really. It's just when you've not had anybody in your corner and when nobody wants to believe you, it's hard. And I didn't really think that I would have that experience. Yet, once she started having all these problems, and I tried to get somebody to help us, there was nobody," she murmured. "Nobody gave a shit, and, once the authorities did their *investigation*," she said, with an eye roll, "there was nothing any of us could do to really help Michelle. Moscow was already so entrenched into her mind that, even though he's long gone now, his torture still remains."

"And that sounds absolutely terrible," Mountain said.

"It is, and why that asshole should be allowed to continue to ruin all these people's lives, I don't understand." She scrubbed her face. "And now sleep couldn't be further off after that phone call."

He nodded. "I'm sorry that it just adds to all the stress you're under."

"What else is new?" she quipped.

"What about at work? Any stress there?"

She shook her head. "No more than usual. You know you have so many hours where you must be polite and keep up professional appearances at all times. The tourists come here to have fun, to let off some steam, and to make some money. They really aren't interested in listening to rules."

"Anybody in particular who caused trouble?"

She shook her head. "No. However, a couple guys I really enjoyed because they were nice and polite and always friendly," she noted, "but you know, most of the time, it's just a job. I'm there until I'm no longer there."

"Got it," he acknowledged.

"And nobody stands out. Just a couple nice guys but that's it."

"I'm surprised the nice guys stand out because the environment is so overcrowded, noisy, and full of the gambling spirit."

"Anything separate from that *does* stand out," she stated.

"Do you have any names for these guys?"

"How would I have names?" she asked, bewildered.

"If I pointed them out to you on a video, would you recognize them?"

"Sure," she replied. "But they won't be the guys you're looking for."

"Why's that?" he asked.

"Because they're nice guys. They're not the ones who turn around and slice people's throats for a few thousand dollars."

He looked at her and gave her a hard knowing look. "Honest to God, I've seen people slice throats for a cup of coffee, so nothing surprises me anymore."

AIDEN WALKED AWAY from his Jeep in complete darkness, totally comfortable in a world without lights. Once he got away from the strip, Aiden really appreciated the normal streetlights, instead of the neon blaring in his face to *Come party all night long*. He hated that whole Vegas strip environment. It was one thing to come for a holiday and to watch the evening shows and to enjoy some gambling, but it was another thing entirely to have it shoved down your face.

It wasn't a place where he could ever live full-time. But, as an employer, the casinos required an awful lot of people in the city. And, as employees, they needed the income.

Aiden made it up to the apartment building in question, pulled out the duplicate key from where he'd been told it was hidden, and let himself into Moscow's apartment. As Aiden stepped inside, he listened to see if anybody was here, but it was empty. And such a hollowness filled it. He flipped on the lights and looked around, but no crime scene tape was here—nothing like that. But then it wasn't a crime scene either. It was just the residence of a dead man.

Aiden shook his head at the thought and walked first to the master bedroom. Most secrets would be kept in the bedroom. As he sat down on the bed to look into the night table, the box springs squeaked.

But he kept digging through the night table and found a series of condom packages that looked like jelly and a few other sex toy accoutrements, but nothing that really revealed much as to his murder. At the base of the night table was an open shelf, holding a couple books, but they looked like they hadn't been touched in a very long time.

"Probably just for show," Aiden said out loud. He knelt, so he could look under the bed, but nothing was there. He lifted the mattress and proceeded to check everything that he could to find anything important or of interest, but nada. He got up, walked to the closet, checked out the wardrobe, and whistled.

Lots of money involved in buying this clothing. Moscow liked to dress up, and he liked to dress well. Aiden always was amazed to see killers or guys full of abuse and drugs, yet who have that whole mentality about trying to pass themselves off as gentlemen. It seemed like they were almost hoping that the clothes would hide who they really were.

And the problem was that they became good at hiding who they were. And the women had no idea of the evil that resided within, until it was too late. It broke Aiden's heart to realize just how badly Toby had been beaten. And that she'd been pressured into marrying Moscow. That she'd gone along with the agreement was another thing that stuck in Aiden's craw.

He shook his head at that and carried on to the other side of the closet. A few things were stuck in the back, and he pulled out a shoe box, expecting to find shoes. However, when he opened it, it was full of cash. He whistled as he looked at it, not sure where any of it had come from. But again, taking your gambling winnings as cash—or spending a lot of time in the casinos, if you're any good at gambling, knowing when to stop and when to move—could have brought Moscow a lot of income. Unreported income.

He took several photos of it and stashed it back into hiding in the closet. Theoretically that cash should belong to Toby now, as his widow, but Aiden didn't know if Moscow had a will that said otherwise.

As Aiden continued his inspection of Moscow's apartment, he didn't find very much else in the bedroom. The bedroom itself was perfectly made up. It had this swinger vibe, with the black satin sheets—that Aiden couldn't imagine would be Toby's style. But then this place didn't have anything to do with her necessarily; it seemed to be more about her being what Moscow wanted.

With a last look, Aiden stepped into the master bathroom, did a quick check, and then headed out to the living room. A small desk sat off to the side. He took a seat, pulled open the desk drawer to find folders upon folders. Frowning at that, he brought out a handful based on the names on those files and took a look inside and just stared. "Good God, talk about finding gold."

He opened them up and took photos, and, just when he was done with the first file and heading into the second, he heard a noise in the outer hallway. Frowning at that, he closed the desk drawer, stood, and stepped behind the front door, still holding the folders of importance. Everything he'd seen so far showed that this Moscow guy was into blackmail, and his blackmail scheme was a bigger source of income for Moscow than probably his gambling was.

But it was also a good way to get himself killed.

All Aiden could think of at this moment in time—as he waited to see where the footsteps outside were leading to— was that this was a hell of a lot stronger motive than a wife who didn't want to be a wife.

Just then Aiden heard voices outside too. "This is the one," a man said outside the door.

Aiden swore softly under his breath and waited. When the doorknob rattled and was found to be locked, he heard tools being brought out, then something inserted into the lock.

Just as he expected the door to open, a woman's voice called out, "Hey, you! What are you doing there?"

# CHAPTER 7

TOBY WOKE FROM a deep sleep with a start. Something was wrong. She looked around the room but couldn't see anything. She turned the lights on but saw nothing wrong. She bolted downstairs, only to have Mountain say in a calm voice, "Hey. What's up?"

She gasped, tried to calm her breathing, and said, "Something is wrong."

He sat up slowly, looked at her, and asked, "In what way? No intruders are here. I haven't heard anything myself to be concerned about."

She stopped and stared. "I can't get rid of that feeling," she explained, and then she spun around in a circle. "Where is Aiden?"

Mountain stood, pulled out his phone, and checked the screen. "He's still at your ex's."

She winced at the term and nodded. "It's him," she said. "Something's wrong with Aiden."

Mountain focused on her curiously.

She couldn't figure out what the hell was wrong, yet the feeling remained. "I don't know what exactly," she cried out. "It's just that feeling."

"Well, I can send him a text, but it might disturb him."

She frowned. "He'll have it on Silent, won't he?"

"He should, but that doesn't mean that it won't vibrate

or do something that could still bring attention to him."

She sagged onto the couch. "Something's wrong," she repeated.

He nodded. "I'll send him a text message." He did, and they both waited, staring at the phone. When no response came, she said, "See? There's a problem."

"Not so sure about that," Mountain countered. "Aiden is a big boy."

"He might be a big boy, but everybody gets into trouble." As he continued to stare at her, she flushed. "I don't know. It just feels like something's wrong."

"And I can go with that, your gut instinct," he confirmed. "I am quite fascinated, however, that you're picking up something on him."

She glared at her cousin. "I like him, but, I mean, obviously we don't have a relationship."

He laughed, lifted his phone, and waggled it at her. "This text right here, if you're correct, is already quite a connection."

She shook her head. "Got nothing to do with him so much as the fact that I just know there's a problem."

"Well, you can delude yourself all you want."

"No deluding," she muttered, staring off in the distance. "I already told you that I like him. But that's a long way away from having a relationship."

"You also don't know what a healthy relationship looks like." At that, she turned and stared. "I mean, Moscow has dominated your world for a very long time."

Her shoulders sagged, and she nodded, her voice barely a whisper. "I know. It's been a really rough time."

"Whereas a relationship with Aiden would be perfectly healthy," he noted in a cheerful voice.

She stared at him. "Are you telling me that you approve of such a thing?" she asked in a mocking tone.

"Absolutely. He'd never do something shitty to you."

"Well, that would be reassuring." Toby studied her cousin intently. "But it's a long way away from you agreeing with something like that."

He smiled. "I'm no longer quite so protective," he explained. "A lot of that back then was just the fact that you were going through a really rough patch with your parents, plus I was going through a really rough patch with my parents. I think it tainted our views of what relationships should be like."

"Yeah. And, of course, you've been just so happy on that relationship roller coaster ride ever since, right?"

"No, not me," he stated. "Not likely to be a relationship in my future either."

"So, why would you want that for me?"

"I wouldn't. I would want something a hell of a lot better," he replied forcefully. "And Aiden is a hell of a lot better."

"Well, Aiden is here to help out. I'm sure he's not thinking about me in that way at all."

At that, her cousin burst out laughing. "He's male. That means he always thinks about it."

She shrugged. "Is that all you guys think about—sex?"

"No, surely not," he teased. "Pizza is at the top of my list too." As he spied the box with the leftovers on the coffee table, he leaned over and grabbed a piece.

"Don't you want to warm that up?" she asked, staring at the congealed cheese, feeling her stomach twist.

"Nope. It's perfectly fine like this. Cold pizza is a food group all unto itself."

"Yeah. One likely to mess up your system."

"Not mine. Again I'm male. We run on this stuff."

She smiled at him. "It really is nice to see you again."

"Good. Once you hook up with Aiden, we'll see each other all the time."

She stared. "Why?"

"Because we're buddies, and we see each other, maybe not as much as we should," Mountain admitted, grimacing. "But, until I get something solved in my life, I can't really be here, having the barbecues in the backyards and lazy Sunday afternoons beside the pool."

"Yet that sounds lovely," she said, with a smile. "And you are right. It's not exactly something we have available for us right now."

"No. But that doesn't mean it isn't what's coming."

After a few minutes of quiet time, she nudged him. "Check your phone."

He looked at her and said, "It hasn't buzzed."

"Check it," she repeated mutinously.

"You're really bothered, aren't you?"

"I am." She jumped to her feet. "Maybe we should go there."

Mountain rose, frowning. "That's not a good idea."

"Leaving him on his own right now is not a good idea either," she said. "Something is wrong."

He frowned, pulled out his phone, and sent another text. "We'll give him another few minutes. … How far away is Moscow's place?"

"About a five-minute drive from here," she stated. "His sister is pretty close as well. All of us live within the same ten-block area. However, if there were a problem, we are just far enough away that we can't get to Aiden fast enough though."

"I trust Aiden to handle whatever he's up against."

"Says you," she said, and she couldn't stop this feeling of danger. It was just getting worse and worse.

Finally Mountain gave in. "Fine. For your sake and your sake only, let's go."

As they went outside, she noted, "We'll have to take my Jeep."

"Good, at least I can sit in that."

She snorted. "I'm not much shorter than you are."

"Oh, hell yes, you are," he argued. "I'm six foot six."

"Okay. Fine, so I'm only five ten and a half."

He smiled. "Has your height ever given you a problem?"

"No, not really." she said, "but it is much nicer to go out with tall guys when you're tall."

"And Aiden is tall," Mountain said, with a cheeky smile. She glared at him, when he added, "Hey, look. We're going to Moscow's. And we're going there right now just because you're afraid something has gone wrong."

"Something *has* gone wrong," she stated, as she reversed the Jeep back down the driveway and headed over to where Aiden should be.

As they got closer, Mountain noted, "Now I don't want you to do anything stupid right now. We'll do a quick reconnaissance first." But, as they pulled up closer, cops were across the street. She gasped and pointed. He nodded grimly. "Cops," he acknowledged, "but no flashing lights. So … what does that mean? They chose to come now and check out Moscow's apartment? Seems rather belated. Does Moscow have more than one place?"

She nodded. "He does. I wonder if the cops didn't know about this one."

"How often did he stay here?"

"Not that often," she said. "He kept rooms right off the strip because of the gambling sites. He went back and forth."

"So, maybe this is a secondary place that the cops just discovered."

"I don't even know if his father knows about this one."

"And that would be another reason why maybe the cops just found out about it."

"It could be," she agreed, "but still it's awfully late at night."

"Well, the father has probably already been here or sent them here to do their job."

She nodded. "Which sounds very much like him." As they watched, she added, "No sign of Aiden."

"If he's in the apartment right now, he's in trouble, but again I trust …"

She gasped, then pointed to the second floor, where somebody climbed out the window. He dropped down what looked like a drainpipe to the ground. "Good God, how is that even possible?"

"Well, that's Aiden," Mountain replied, "so it's definitely possible."

As the man bolted around the next building, she immediately started up the Jeep and followed him. "What about his vehicle?"

"It'll be here, not too close by," Mountain noted. And even as he said that, they came around the block to see him hop into the rental. She flashed her headlights at him. He turned, saw them, lifted a hand in a surprise greeting, and pulled up toward them. She pulled up beside him.

Aiden looked at Mountain. "What's the matter?"

Mountain shook his head and pointed. "Her."

At that, Mountain leaned back so that Toby could look

directly at Aiden. "Something was wrong," she stated, staring at him in astonishment. "We came because I insisted."

"Sure, something was wrong," Aiden agreed. "But I'm certainly not used to people coming to help out."

At that, she shrugged.

"Let's talk at home," he said. And with that, he quickly pulled out in front of her.

She followed him back to her place at a more sedate pace. "What kind of a life is it when nobody expects somebody to come and help out?"

"You should know," her cousin said, beside her, "because that's how you've been living too."

And there wasn't a whole lot she could say to that.

AIDEN PULLED UP in the front of Toby's house, hopped out, and walked up to the front door. He was still a little flummoxed at the idea of her forcing Mountain out because she was worried. That would have taken some effort because Mountain was not the kind of guy to panic. As they followed him to the front door, he murmured something along that line to Mountain.

She immediately jumped into the conversation. "He only came because I insisted. Honestly I had just such a strong terrible feeling that I could not just sit around and do nothing."

"Well, much appreciated," Aiden replied. "However, you know if you'd done anything more about it and had gone into the building or had talked to the cops, it could have gotten me in a lot of trouble."

"And I wasn't really thinking of that," she admitted.

"We did see you come out of the building."

"Oh, did you?" He laughed. "Hopefully nobody else did."

Mountain nodded, otherwise silently listening to their exchange.

She shook her head. "I couldn't believe you made that jump."

"Once you slide down the gutter," he explained, "not really much more to it. All depends on how good a job they've done with securing the gutters to the wall. Unfortunately shoddy workmanship means that a tumble is more likely than not."

She shook her head, as she slumped onto the couch and stared at him. "So, nothing was wrong?"

"Sure, something was wrong," he noted. "The cops came. And I didn't have a whole lot of places to go. I was photographing the material in files that your husband had," he added, "and it looks to me very much like blackmail."

"Blackmail?" she asked in astonishment.

"Yes," Aiden confirmed. "I've got a ton of photos to download onto my laptop. And I took away a little black book." He held it up.

"Wow. Are you allowed to do that?" she asked him.

"No security was in that building. You, as his widow, technically own the apartment, so I figured that anything inside it should have been fair game too."

"Why would I own it? Oh God." She stared at him in shock. "That's probably another reason why his father would be fighting hard to make these charges stick."

"That's right. Unless we hear differently, everything in Moscow's estate is left to you," he noted, with a smile. "And, if a lot is involved, then Moscow's father won't want to share."

"No, he won't. And he'll make my life very difficult in the meantime."

"Yeah, he's really not a nice guy, is he?"

She shook her head. "No, he's not, and he's all about the money. But then you know that's how he created a son in his image, so they certainly understood each other."

"In this case," Aiden said, "it's not always a good thing. But we will get to the bottom of this."

"Do you think the cops will keep that evidence?"

"I didn't think so," he replied, pulling files from underneath his jacket. "These were inside his desk. If he had multiple homes, no telling where more of the like could be— or just duplicates for safekeeping."

She nodded, then frowned. "I do have a bunch of stuff he left here, but I didn't even think of it."

"Where is it?" Aiden asked.

"In the garage," she murmured. At that, she got up, walked to the kitchen, opened up the connecting garage door, and turned on the light. She pointed to a couple boxes put off to the side.

"And you don't know what's in these?" Aiden asked.

"He made it very clear that I wasn't to have anything to do with the boxes. He was just storing this stuff for a friend. Had nothing to do with him."

"Well, what do you want to bet it has to do with the fact that he may have had a good idea that he was in trouble," Aiden murmured. "Nice guy to bring that danger to you though." Both Aiden and Mountain headed to the boxes, picked them up and carried them into the living room.

With the garage locked again behind her, she said, "I don't understand what or who he'd be blackmailing."

"In a city like this, it could be any number of things or people," Aiden suggested. As he started to sift through the files, he noted, "This looks like copies of what I was trying to get photos of before the cops came."

"Well, that's good that we have duplicates," she said. "Isn't it?"

"Yeah, it is," he agreed. "It means that the cops won't bury it, and, sure enough, another little black book is here too." He held it up and tossed it to her. "Do you know any of these names?"

"There aren't any names here," she replied. "These appear to be just numbers."

"It's probably a code," Mountain guessed. "Remember how your father had that problem in the casino way back when? About this group of young guys from the university who were cheating by using code words or special body language that they tossed back-and-forth in a game?"

"Yeah." Toby nodded. "God, I don't remember how that even worked, but they were doing something shady like that, and that's how they caught them."

"Right. Well, take a look at those numbers. It looks like a code to me."

"Doesn't mean it's connected though."

"No. I'm not saying it is," Aiden stated. "I'm just saying that your husband—

"My ex-husband," she corrected him in a firm voice. When he turned his focus on her, she sighed. "Fine, okay my husband. But I'm a widow now so ..."

"Right," he agreed. "A moot point anyway. He looks like he was making a lot of money off these people."

"I just don't know who these people would be," she said.

"What they are now are leads for who would have killed

him," he replied. "Anybody who deals in blackmail makes enemies. That completely widens the suspect pool as to who could have killed Moscow. And whether the cops like it or not, they can't hide this."

"And yet they probably won't take it into account," she complained bitterly.

"Did you ever get that lawyer process taken care of?" Aiden asked. "That's something where your lawyer will go to bat for you to get all the charges dropped."

"They won't drop any charges," Mountain said, "not until we have something a little stronger than this."

"You mean the fact that he was blackmailing people isn't enough?" Toby asked her cousin.

"No. It would just be potentially more motive on your part. You could keep all this money and keep up the blackmail scheme and not have to share."

She stared at Mountain. "That's disgusting."

His lips twitched. "Maybe, but that's how the world works," he stated. "You are already assumed guilty, so what we have to do is prove that you're innocent."

She shook her head. "That's not even possible with these dirty cops doing favors for Moscow's dad."

"Sure, it is possible," Mountain argued. "We're well on our way to proving your innocence. We just have to keep digging."

"I still can't believe Moscow was blackmailing people," she murmured. "I mean, I knew he was a lowlife but—"

"And a lowlife with a very dangerous pastime that brought him a lot of money," Aiden noted, pulling out bank statements. "He has a separate bank account here, and the income is sometimes $20,000 up to sometimes $50,000 a month."

She stared at him in shock. "Did you say, a month?"

He nodded and handed her the statement.

She looked over it and shook her head. "I've never even seen anything like this."

"Well, he also had a big box of money there at his apartment," he added. "I took photos of it." He pulled out his phone and held it up for her to see.

She shook her head. "Could be $20,000 or $30,000 right there."

"Yeah, I would say so," he murmured.

"Hang on a minute. The guys who were at his apartment, who were they?" she asked.

"They were supposedly cops, but the older lady across the hall accosted them and demanded to see their badges. She said that nobody was going in there and that she'd already called the real cops, and, if these guys didn't have ID, they better get the hell out of there."

"Nice," Toby said, with a huge grin.

"In other words"—Aiden turned toward Mountain—"I did get out of there without her or the fake cops seeing me, but we need to go back to the apartment and clean it out."

Mountain nodded. "Good idea." He checked his watch. "And we're not leaving her alone."

"Right," Toby agreed. "I have to come with you. Where there is money, people are coming after it."

He nodded. "But you seem to have the legal right to it."

She winced. "Not only that, I think I have keys." She got up, walked over to the sideboard, and pointed. "He dropped these in this box a while ago. I didn't even know what they were for. He didn't tell me."

Aiden studied the keys and nodded. "Looks like a safe deposit box key and also a storage locker key." He glanced at

Mountain.

"I'm on it. I'll ask Corbin to get the team on it."

She shook her head as she stared at it. "Why didn't he make things clear?"

"He knew you would figure it out. And he never really expected to die, but this was kind of a 'just in case' backup for him. And he could always pick up the boxes and the keys and take them away from you later. You were already under his thumb enough that, if you didn't listen, he would just beat the crap out of you again, and then you would listen next time."

She stared at Aiden, then nodded. "And you know something? I wouldn't have touched anything anyway. He terrified me at all times."

"However, by being his legal wife, you probably own all this, what with the Nevada inheritance laws, unless some Last Will and Testament says otherwise," Mountain mentioned.

Aiden nodded. "I don't trust people, so why don't we head over there and grab anything valuable? And make sure you bring your wedding certificate with you."

She stared at him in shock. "Why?"

"Because you have a nosy neighbor," he explained, with a smile, "and she might want to sit there and give you big congrats on your nuptials."

# CHAPTER 8

A S ALL THREE of them headed back to her ex's place, Aiden gave them a heads-up about what he had already found, what they should each look for.

Toby said, "Doesn't it seem like we're doing everything backward?"

"It certainly never occurred to any of us," Aiden replied from the back seat of her Jeep, "that the cops wouldn't have already been there to check out a dead guy's apartment."

She shook her head. "It certainly didn't occur to me because I was trying to avoid thinking about him at all."

"However, we need to strip everything from there while we can."

"You don't think they were really cops?"

"No, I don't think they were really cops," Aiden noted. "And I wouldn't be at all surprised if they aren't back now."

The trio returned to the apartment in no time. Toby brought out the duplicate keys she had and unlocked Moscow's apartment. Sure enough, the ever-watchful neighbor came out into the hallway. She looked at her in astonishment, saw the key in her hand, and queried, "Who are you?"

"I'm his widow," Toby explained. "And, if I understand correctly from one of the other neighbors, some people were trying to get in here earlier tonight. I had deliberately not cleaned out Moscow's stuff yet, but now I'm wondering if I should be looking after something in here."

The woman immediately nodded. "Oh my, yes," she replied. "They were trying to tell me they were cops, but they didn't look like any cops I know." She shook her head. "My husband was on the force for a long time. I know what cops look like." She looked at the other two men with Toby suspiciously.

At that, Aiden smiled gently and said, "Good evening, ma'am. Thank you so much for looking after her place."

"I don't think I've ever met you," she replied hesitantly, her gaze fell on Toby first, then going from one person to the other.

"Then you don't gamble," she noted, with a smile.

"No. Of course not," she stated. "That's a waste of money."

"Agreed, but unfortunately it's also a place where I needed to work. Moscow and I were childhood sweethearts," Toby explained.

The woman's eyes opened wide. "That's where I've seen you before. I was in his apartment once, and he has pictures of you all over the place."

All she could do was to keep smiling. "And it's been a devastating couple weeks."

"Oh, my dear, I'm so sorry. He was always really good to me, you know?"

And, with that, Toby swung open the door. Them having the keys seemed to satisfy the older lady, as she returned to her apartment. Aiden walked over to her and said, "You mentioned that they didn't look like cops. Do you know what they looked like?"

"I took a picture of them," she replied proudly.

He looked at her in fascination. "I don't suppose I could see those pictures, could I?"

"Sure, you can," she agreed. "You're helping her, so that means it's her apartment." The older woman sent a dubious look toward Toby, but she'd already gone inside.

Toby popped her head outside the door and added, "Yes, it was Moscow's apartment, and I'm his wife."

"Right," the older woman said. "Sorry. You get to be very suspicious in this world."

"And sometimes it's necessary," Toby noted.

"All the time it's necessary," she murmured. "It just seems like everybody is out to cheat or to steal from one another. I don't know what the world has come to."

She pulled up her phone, and, with an adeptness that surprised Aiden, she brought up the picture she took. He looked at the photos and then back at her and nodded. "Any chance I could have a copy of these, so I could take it to the police?"

"I did phone the police, and I did show these to them," she stated. "But you know? The real police didn't seem to care very much either." And between the two of them, they managed to get the photos transferred to his phone.

He smiled. "Thank you very much, ma'am. Now I'll go in and help Toby."

"That's right," she confirmed, the last of her doubts falling away from her facial expression. "It was Toby. I always thought Toby was a male, but he always talks about Toby."

"That's his wife," Aiden stated. "They have another place, where she's been staying this whole time. They only got married a couple weeks ago. He was killed soon afterward, which is why you haven't seen very much of her."

"Oh, that poor child!" she murmured in horror. "This is

just such a terrible world we live in now. Nobody seems to want to help one another. Everybody is just after money." She shook her head. "My poor dear Willie would be turning over in his grave."

"Well, you've done a good deed tonight," Aiden said, "and we appreciate it." And, with that, he headed back to Moscow's apartment. When Aiden turned, the older lady finally seemed satisfied that they were where they belonged and had gone inside her own apartment. As he stepped inside, Toby stood in the middle of the living room, staring at something Aiden had yet to mention to her—a life-size photograph of her on the wall.

"That is so creepy," she whispered to him.

"Well, I can tell you that, whatever feelings Moscow had for you, they were very complex. Nobody does something like this without being very involved, one way or another."

"You know what? I think, in his own psychotic way, he probably loved me," she noted, "but his version of love is not what most people would call it."

"No. And that is unfortunately often the way of it," he murmured. "Now, before we end up with cops and various other entities around here, let's start getting some of this stuff out of here, particularly the files." And he pointed to the cases that he had found earlier in the desk.

At that, Mountain searched the kitchen for some plastic bags and quick loaded up some files and started carrying them out.

"Where's the money?" she asked.

"In the closet."

And, with that, they headed to the closet, pulled out the shoebox, but then she pointed to another box farther back. "Can you reach that?" she asked.

Aiden nodded, pulled it down, and then was stunned. Inside was a weapon—a Smith & Wesson handgun. "Did he have a license for this?"

She stared at it. "I have no idea. Yet I have seen that gun before though."

He stared at her. "What?"

"He was playing with it and threatening me with it," she stated, a shudder running through her body. "I forgot all about it until now."

"Nobody like Moscow should have a gun."

"No. Maybe he shouldn't have, but that doesn't mean that that's the way the world works."

Aiden nodded. "I'll take it, and we'll run the ballistics on it and see if it's been used in any shootings."

"Good idea," she agreed. "I know I don't want it. I don't know if we should turn it in to the cops."

"I'll handle it," Aiden replied immediately. "We also have a lot of files here we need to go through and need to contact the police about."

"You'll have to do that because you know the cops won't believe anything I have to say."

"Well, the good thing is," Aiden noted, "we have some contacts. And we'll find somebody honest within this town who can deal with this."

She stared at him. "Do you really think anybody honest is left?"

He smiled gently, wrapped an arm around her shoulders, and gave her a quick hug. "It's been a rough couple weeks for you," he noted, "but remember. The cavalry is here." Matter of fact, he had a lot that he would take to the police. He wanted clearance from Corbin as to who was not corrupt and thus safe to go to. Of course nobody ever knew for sure who wasn't dirty, but Aiden was prepared to put his trust in Corbin to find out.

Before they left Moscow's apartment this time, they must have all the valuables and information removed first. Aiden looked around the rest of the apartment and asked, "Any idea what you want to do with the rest of this?"

She shook her head. "I'm pretty sure Moscow's father will have something to say about this too," she stated, "and it won't be friendly."

He looked at her. "Meaning?"

"You heard me. Meaning that he'll say it's all his."

"Well, you don't want any of it, do you?"

"No, I don't," she said. "I want the files and the money obviously." She stopped and added, "Moscow always mentioned something about pictures."

At that, they headed to the photos on the wall and studied them. "I don't know anything about art," Aiden admitted. "I don't recognize any of these photos—other than yours of course—or the artwork, and I don't know anything about the artists involved."

Mountain arrived to join the discussion. "No, I don't either, but that doesn't necessarily mean that's what Moscow was talking about." Mountain lifted the first frame, took it off the wall, put it back on again, and systematically they looked behind each one. In the bedroom, Mountain lifted one and said, "It's here."

At that, they removed the artwork to find a wall safe. She looked at it in shock. "I didn't even know he had a safe," she noted.

"Maybe not, but did he at any time give you anything that would make you think you could open this?"

She looked at him and pointed out the glass bowl in

front of them. "Unless something in there is the clue."

Aiden nodded. "Got it. Let me see." He stepped forward, and, within minutes, he had the wall safe open. She stared at him, frowning. He pointed to the bowl, holding three numbered pool balls. "It's the combination. So, looking at the pool balls he put in there, it was just a matter of getting them in the right order."

She shook her head. "I'm almost getting the idea that he wanted me to find this."

"I think he did want you to find it, if he didn't live, but I don't think he wanted you to know anything about it as long as he was alive."

"And that makes sense," she agreed. "I wasn't to know anything ever. I wasn't to ask questions. As he was concerned, everything was on a need-to-know basis."

"And now you need to know." With that, Aiden stepped aside and pointed. "Go ahead."

She looked at the safe with misgivings. "Are you sure I have any right to this?"

"You are the deceased's wife. This is one of the two properties that we know of that he had in his holdings," Aiden explained. "I would definitely want to open that safe."

"Well, I want to open it," she said, "but it feels more like Pandora's box."

"After everything else we found so far?" he asked, with a note of amusement.

"Right, that's just being foolish." She stepped forward, turned the handle, and popped it open. And inside was money, like a lot of money. "Dear God," she whispered.

Aiden nodded. "This is coming with us. No way in hell we're leaving this. That could have been what the fake cops were looking for." He looked around, grabbed a travel bag from the closet, and nodded to Mountain. "Let's get this loaded up."

"And what are the chances there's more?" Toby asked.

"You did find a safe deposit key and that locker key, so my bet is on more money will be found there too. I already have Corbin and the team working on matching up the keys with the institutions," Mountain noted, as he started moving the money bundles into the travel bag.

Aiden looked over at her. "Was he lucky at the tables?"

She nodded. "Sometimes he was very lucky, yet he also seemed to know when to walk away."

"And, of course, that's always a huge factor," he murmured. "Those guys who can't walk away end up in trouble."

"And I see that all the time at my table," she agreed. "I just didn't think Moscow was holding this kind of money."

"How did he feel about banks?"

She winced. "He didn't trust them. Then he didn't trust cops either."

"With good reason apparently," Aiden noted. "If you think about it so far, none of the cops have been terribly helpful."

"No. And I'm wondering about that again. I think that's just his father's influence over the dirty cops."

"And yet I know more about Moscow just from what I see here," Aiden stated.

She nodded. "I know, and it's given me a completely different view of him. Something was very sick about the way he looked at me."

He nodded. "He must have done the same thing with the huge picture of you on the wall."

She shuddered at that. "To even think that he was looking at that on a regular basis? Just creeps me out."

"And yet you had a history that went way back."

"We did," she admitted soberly. "It was a history I did my best to erase. But he wasn't having anything to do with it."

"And how much did his sister have to do with any of it?"

She shook her head. "I've known her for as long as him obviously," she explained. "Of course I'm much closer to her versus the rest of Moscow's family."

"And I gather his father doesn't like you."

"No," she confirmed, "and then he probably has full justification in his mind. I tattled about the treatment that poor Michelle was getting."

"Good," Aiden said.

"Sure," she said, "*good* in the sense that I was trying to defend her, but it was definitely a mouse going up against a lion."

He nodded. "And unfortunately that happens, and lions don't like to give up their place."

She laughed. "For all I know, this lion is involved in this."

"You think so?" Mountain asked, as he checked once again to make sure nothing else remained in the safe.

"You know what he's like," she stated, turning to look at her cousin.

He nodded. "He's slimy, but he has this steady stream of friends."

"Are they friends though?" Aiden asked. "We all know people who hang on because there is his money to enjoy."

SATISFIED THAT MOSCOW'S apartment yielded no more

surprise secrets, they made it back to her place. Aiden stepped outside on the deck and called Corbin. When his sleepy voice answered, Aiden smiled and said, "Twenty-four hours a day."

"Yeah, I'm here." Corbin yawned. "What's up?" When Aiden filled Corbin in about what they'd found, Corbin became wide awake in a jolt. "Blackmail money, as in, how much money?"

"Hundreds and hundreds of thousands of dollars," Aiden replied, "if the blackmail folders hold true. I don't know how this money gets divided in a state like Nevada, but Toby seems to stand to gain a lot of money."

"Which won't make her look very credible either."

"I know. Every time we find something that shows Moscow to be a piece of shit, it also shows that she had a lot more motives for killing him."

"Right," Corbin agreed. "Sucks to be her at the moment."

"And yet I don't think she had anything to do with that."

"No, I don't either," Corbin confirmed. "Oh, by the way. We traced the two keys. One to a safe deposit box in a big bank nearby and the other to one of the storage lots, also in Vegas. My vote is that they are both full of money. I didn't want to pull you guys off Toby alibi duty, so I've asked a local retired navy guy I trust to fill in for us here. He'll let me know what he finds. But again, instead of getting proof that she's innocent, we keep finding more things that the cops could use to show that she isn't."

"I also have a Smith & Wesson that we found in Moscow's closet, and I want a contact in the Vegas police I can take this gun to who's honest. She's been charged with murder, and anything that she does will make it look worse to those dirty cops."

"You're right," Corbin agreed. "Let me think about that, and I'll call you back."

Aiden got off the phone and sat down on the chair outside.

Almost immediately Toby stepped out, looked at him, and asked, "Is it safe to come outside?"

He looked at her and nodded. "Yes, of course."

"I heard you on the phone and didn't want to interrupt," she added.

"I asked my boss for somebody honest at this station to turn in the gun to."

"Oh, that'd be interesting," she said, with a smile. "You know that all this just gives them more motivation for thinking that I did this."

"Of course it does when they are focused on only you," he noted. "Makes me wonder if your husband didn't plan for you to look guilty, should he die under suspicious circumstances."

"And you know something? He was just enough of a shit to have done something like that," she admitted, "but I don't know. … That picture of me on the wall? It gives me a completely different view of him."

"Yet it doesn't endear you more to him?"

"Hell no," she repeated flatly. "He's still the asshole who held that gun to my head and beat the crap out of me and terrorized Michelle."

"Speaking of Michelle," Aiden noted, "if I went to talk to her, would she tell me much?"

"I don't know," Toby replied. "I'm not sure the cops have ever talked to her."

He nodded. "Maybe that's something that we should do," he suggested. "I don't want to upset her is the only thing."

"Well, she's been so upset over all this. At this point, maybe it'd be better to upset her now and get it over with."

He understood what she was trying to say and wasn't sure if he agreed or not, but it was definitely something to consider.

When Aiden's phone rang again, Corbin said, "I'll text you a name and a number of an honest detective. Contact him privately first."

"Got it," Aiden replied, and, with that, he hung up. He stared at his phone, until it buzzed and the text came in. "Now we have a name and a phone number," he told Toby.

"You won't call him this late tonight, will you?"

"No. Not a good way to start off a new relationship," he agreed, with a smile, looking down at his watch. "It's like one o'clock in the morning."

"*Ugh.*" She shrugged. "Yet it's not as if I'm going anywhere tomorrow."

"No, not at the moment. Do you want to stay in Vegas when this is over?" he asked her, looking at her curiously.

She shrugged. "I don't know that I do. Yet I don't know that I don't. With Michelle here, I don't really have any reason to go anywhere else, unless this murder investigation really taints my reputation in town."

"And what about your parents?"

"They'd be fine if I left completely," she stated flatly. "Remember that whole 'I'm a troublemaker' thing?"

He shook his head. "You know that just blows me away that anybody could even think that. It's hardly your fault that Moscow's death is being pinned on you."

"Well, according to my parents, it's all my fault. And, if they get any bad publicity out of this, it'll be my fault all over again."

"Well, I hope they get whatever is coming to them," he replied.

At that, Mountain stepped outside. He held the black book in his hand. "We might have another reason for your parents' attitude."

She asked, "What's that?"

"They were being blackmailed by Moscow." She stared at him, clearly shocked. He held up the book and added, "Their names are in here."

"But do we know that the little black book only deals with blackmail?" she asked curiously. "And what could Moscow possibly have on them?"

"According to this black book, we're supposed to check a file number." And he read it off.

"Oh, good. Moscow was organized." Aiden got up and bolted to the files. He quickly pulled out the corresponding file, read the number off again, and nodded. "This one."

"Yeah, that's it." Mountain nodded. "Look at that. It's even got your father's name on it." With them crowding around, Aiden quickly flipped through the file. "Well, what do you know?" he said. "Your daddy is having an affair."

"Yeah, I can't see that that'd be something worth blackmailing over," Toby countered, with a snort. "My mom never cared, as long as he didn't involve her."

"Ah, that may be," Aiden noted. "However, would she feel the same way if it got out that he was having an affair with a guy?" And he held up the photo of her father and some other man, both nude and entwined in a lover's embrace.

# CHAPTER 9

TOBY STARED AT Aiden in shock. "My father in a homosexual relationship?" She shook her head. "No way my mother would tolerate that."

At that, even Mountain snorted. "No, she'd be screaming from the treetops."

"So now you know why he paid Moscow to keep it quiet."

"Oh, yes. Wow. Okay. How the high and mighty have fallen," she said, casting a glance at Mountain.

"It's his life," her cousin noted, "but, once you get into the blackmail trap, it doesn't really end."

Toby nodded. "And, of course, Moscow knew he was my father, so that would have made turning the screw a little bit more fun for him."

"Did your father know that you had a strange relationship with Moscow?"

"Yes, because we've been more or less in a strange relationship since we were teens in school," she replied. "Particularly my mother knew and gave me holy hell."

"Then, yes, Moscow probably had a lot of fun applying that kind of pressure to your parents," Aiden suggested. "On the other hand, Moscow's the one who's dead, and, unfortunately at this point in time, the cops need to take a look at this and see who was being blackmailed."

"Right. And, of course, my parents will blame me for that again too."

He nodded. "I suspect that they probably will. But these files give away a lot of other people's secrets as well."

"You know what? Maybe it is time to leave this town." She looked at the blackmail files. "I mean, when people realize we were married and that we found all this, will they think they're safe, or will they come after me now?"

"It's one of the reasons," Aiden explained, "that I wondered if you wanted to stay here."

"I've been telling her for a long time that she should leave," Mountain added.

"And go where?" she asked, with a challenge to her voice. "It's not as if I have very much in the way of options."

"Well," Mountain began, "I won't be around for a while, with this other op. So, if you wanted to, you could have my place while I'm gone." She looked at him suspiciously. He nodded and continued. "I know. I can't tell you anything about where I'm going and why, but I did tell Aiden here that he had me for just until the end of tomorrow. Then possibly I would leave."

"We don't have any more time to lose then," she snapped. "What else can we learn here?"

"First, sleep," Aiden declared. She stared at him. He shook his head. "You can only function for so long without rest."

"Well, I can function a whole lot longer, considering that I am under a murder charge." However, even with that added impetus, she was losing the argument and knew it.

Mountain shook his head at her. "No. You get some sleep. We all need some sleep."

She looked at her cousin and asked him, "Will you stand

guard?"

"We should," Aiden agreed, "but I suspect we're both equally tired. Toby, do you have a scanner here at home?"

She shook her head.

"No matter. I'll take pics of these blackmail files with my phone if need be. So I'll be up for a while doing that. Plus we don't have a credible threat."

"In theory," Mountain added, "but I'll stay down here, just in case."

"Well, you would do that anyway though," Aiden teased.

"I would," he agreed cheerfully. "However, you both need to go to bed." With that, he turned Toby in the direction of the stairs and said, "Go." And she went.

Upstairs, she struggled into a camisole, brushed her teeth, and crashed on her bed. She really was exhausted, but she had so much going on in her head that she didn't know what to even think of it all. Hearing Aiden coming up the stairs, she realized she hadn't asked him if he needed anything. She stepped out into the hallway. "Hey. Do you want a shower or something? Do you need towels?"

He gave her a wave of his hand. "I'm fine. I need sleep first and so will recharge and pick this up in the morning."

"Do you think everything here is safe?"

"It is," he said.

"Not if somebody saw us leave Moscow's apartment," she noted. "I mean, if it were me, I'd burn this place down." He stared at her, and she shrugged. "Yeah. I have a strong mind-set when it comes to crap like this."

"No, it's an interesting thought," he murmured. "It's also why Mountain will sleep downstairs."

"Still the fact remains that only you and I are up here,"

she quipped in a teasing voice.

He nodded. "Good point, but rest is what we both need."

And his tone was gentle enough that she could only agree. "I'll see you in the morning then." And, with that, she went back to bed, but she found it almost impossible to sleep. She was too keyed up. Too much information floated through her brain, and, when she did finally crash, it was hours later. When she woke the next morning, it was way later than she had expected it to be. She jumped to her feet, dressed, and headed to the kitchen. There, the men were already sitting at the kitchen table, working on the blackmail files.

"Well, at least the house didn't burn to the ground last night," she noted cheerfully.

At that, Mountain looked up at her, frowned, and asked, "What's that?"

She pointed to Aiden and explained, "We were just talking last night about, you know, burning this place to the ground would be an easy way to get rid of all the evidence." Mountain stared at her. She shrugged. "Okay. Fine, it was a bit of a late-night lack-of-sleep joke."

"Regardless, not exactly a joke," Mountain replied, "but you're right. It would have been a hell of a way to burn up all the evidence, plus all of us, so let's consider it our good fortune that we made it through the night. Let's not even entertain that thought."

"Or," she added, "we get copies of all this, send it to the cloud, take it all to the cops, and see what they can make of it."

"That's the plan," Aiden confirmed from beside her. She realized he had files open and was snapping photos of each page with his phone, filling in digital copies of what he didn't have already.

"That's still all the blackmail stuff?"

"Oh, yeah. I'm getting copies of every page of it."

"And isn't that what blackmailers are always terrified of?" she asked curiously. "That somebody—other than the person blackmailing them—will get copies of what they're trying hard to keep secret?"

"Absolutely," Aiden agreed. "And, once this goes to the cops, you know it'll be hard to keep it contained."

She shrugged. "So what? Am I supposed to go to jail on a trumped-up murder charge while my father protects his affair? No, that's hardly justice."

"Maybe not, but there could be a lot of hard feelings when this comes out."

"Well, it's not my hard feelings," she declared. "As much as I wouldn't want to drag my parents through anything, I also don't owe them anything, and I didn't partake in that affair nor that blackmail scheme," she stated. "I've got enough on my plate that I'm trying to deal with on my own. I'm not worrying about them too."

"Did you ever wonder if your parents thought you knew about Moscow blackmailing them and thought you were a party to this?" Mountain asked her.

She stared at him, as she brought her coffee over to the table. "First, I don't think Mom knows about Dad's affair, or she would have divorced him quick and got away from the affair before they got outed. That way Mommy dearest could say the affair came after their failed marriage."

Mountain nodded. "Sounds like your mom."

"So I just think Dad was making the blackmail payments, keeping that from Mom. For all we know, Dad didn't know who he was making the blackmail payments to, right?" she replied. "We haven't had this stuff in our possession long enough to even think about the consequences of it. But, if my father had any thoughts along that line, that would explain why he's being so cold."

"Not really," Mountain argued, shaking his head, "that's just your dad."

"And all that gushing over with compliments for Moscow all these years by my parents? Was that all forced due to the blackmail?" She groaned as she sat down. "Why are people so strange?"

"Because they're unhappy for one," Aiden suggested. "I mean, if your dad is homosexual, stuck in a marriage he hates, and has now been paying blackmail to cover his affair that he would prefer to live fully, then you know he's living a double life and obviously hates it."

She stared at him. "It never even occurred to me that he would have this kind of relationship with somebody."

"Does it bother you?" Aiden asked her.

"It bothers me in the sense that he has been living a lie. Does it bother me that he had a homosexual relationship? Of course not. As long as he's not hurting anybody, I don't think it matters. But obviously he was hurting somebody—my mother. But then I'm not sure that my mother even knows—or counts," she stated, with a wry tone. "You have to meet my mother in order to understand why I say that."

"No, but I would agree," Mountain confirmed. "Enough's going on here right now that'll be hard to keep track of it all. And I'm sure your father and Moscow's other blackmail victims are all trying to figure out where their future in all this is, now that Moscow's dead. They may probably think they're off the hook, but there'll be that terrible feeling in their stomachs, wondering if somebody else will start up the blackmail again. Not to mention the fact that the cops will have to look at all these blackmail victims closely, as being really good suspects for Moscow's murder."

"Do you think my esteemed *father-in-law* knew about the blackmail?" she asked the guys.

"It depends how much alike father and son are," Aiden noted. "Sometimes, something like that would bond father and son, particularly power plays that turn up—like finding out about your father and his affair. Just think about it. Did the blackmail victims know who was blackmailing them? Or was it some clandestine email with incriminating pics and a drop location noted, with the amount due in cash at whatever date and time?"

Aiden raised an eyebrow and continued. "If so, then every time Moscow would run across your father, Moscow would secretly know, and this would give him great pleasure. And, of course, Moscow could always have those double-entendre conversations that would make your father wonder if Moscow knew something. Hell, could be such conversations between the two dads even. Regardless, your father would know Moscow and his dad were related."

"Right," she said. "That just sounds terrible to further taunt their victims."

"It does sound terrible, but it's not your responsibility."

"And yet somehow," she added, "it feels very much like it's, you know, mud on my own fingers."

"But it isn't. This is not your deal," Aiden stated. "Remember that."

THEY WERE MULLING over everything, while Aiden took his photos, and suddenly he said, "Okay, I'm done." He looked over at Mountain. "I feel like I should call this detective now, the one Corbin recommended."

"Call him and set up a meeting," Mountain stated. "That would be the simplest."

"Right, and then we have to take all this shit to him."

"I would think so."

"What about my lawyer? Should I contact him and let him know?"

"It wouldn't hurt," Aiden replied. "Do you want to do that with all of us here?"

She frowned as she thought about that and nodded. "I never really know how to handle this kind of stuff. So, if at least you're here, maybe I'll just phone him," she suggested, looking at Aiden.

"Yes," Aiden agreed. "That would work."

At that, she made the midmorning phone call to her lawyer, put her phone on Speaker. When he answered in a sleepy voice, she explained everything they'd found at her husband's apartment.

Her lawyer was jovial about it all. "You get that to the cops," he said, "and I'll come in and get all the charges dropped."

"Nothing clears me though," she stated.

"No, but an awful lot more suspects are now available for them to look at, and they need to be looking at them now," he noted, "before they come back after you."

She nodded. "I know that we're supposed to go meet somebody today with all this stuff."

"Good," her attorney said, and then his voice changed. "Who are you taking it to?"

She looked over at Aiden.

Aiden shook his head.

"I'm not sure. Aiden and Mountain have somebody honest they're supposed to deal with. I think that appointment has already been set up."

"Good," he said. "Let me know when you guys are back, and it's all clear for me to approach the cops."

"Did you want copies of all this?"

"We'll keep copies of it," he stated, his tone brisk, "just in case the authorities get difficult. But I'm not expecting any further problems from them."

"Okay, I'm glad to hear that," she said, with relief. When she hung up, she looked over at Aiden. "That sounds pretty solid."

"Yeah. He also can't make a claim like that though," Mountain countered, with a wry tone. "Only the cops can drop the charges, and, at this point in time, I'm not so willing to believe that they will do so."

She looked at him. "That's because I'm still the number one suspect, right?"

"Yeah," he agreed, "you are, and you're not getting out of that spot until we find out who killed those guys."

"Right." She brushed her hair off her face, then turned toward Aiden. "When do you want to go meet the detective?"

"Now," he replied calmly, "and the sooner, the better."

"Are we going to the police station?"

"No, we're not," Aiden noted. "We'll meet at his house."

At that, she shook her head. "That doesn't sound kosher."

"It's a hell of a lot more kosher than giving it to the dirty cops who are likely to bury it."

"Oh, crap," she muttered. "Fine. And do we have a copy of it all?"

"Yes," Aiden confirmed. "I've got copies downloading to my laptop. Once I have a chance to check them over, we're out of here." He sat before his laptop and quickly flicked through every photo.

She looked over the files and then at Mountain. "What about the money?" she asked.

Mountain said, "We'll tell them about the money, but it was in Moscow's apartment, and it's none of their business, outside of the fact that you did find cash money. I mean, Moscow was a known gambler. That cash could have been his gambling winnings, not necessarily blackmail payments."

"Okay." She sighed, and then she asked a question that had been on her mind all night. "However, do *you* think it's blackmail money?"

"I don't know if it's blackmail money or his winnings," Mountain admitted. "As you already told us, Moscow often won at the casino."

"And that's true," she noted. "I've seen him do it time and time again."

"Do you think he cheated?"

"No. I think he was just naturally lucky. He used to tell me how he would know when it was important to go play and when it wasn't. He also knew when it was time to quit. If he lost three times, he was done. But, if he lost twice and then won the next time, he'd keep going until he lost three times. It was a simple system, but it worked for him. And I have seen him clean up tens of thousands at a time."

"So, in that case," Aiden added, "we can't be sure where that money came from."

"I just wondered if I'm supposed to return it to the people he blackmailed."

"Would you want to give that money—say, whatever your dad supposedly paid—back to him?"

She stared at him and winced. "And that would mean facing him about his affair too, wouldn't it?"

"It would, indeed," Aiden agreed. "And we also don't know what happened to that money—where it went, what Moscow did with it, and whether he even got it. Just because he was blackmailing people doesn't automatically mean anybody paid Moscow. We don't have dates on any of these blackmail schemes. We're still a long way from ciphering it all out," Aiden explained. "So, hold your horses on feeling guilty."

"Well, it's guilt, and also that sense of 'If I want to get out of here, I need money to leave with.' And I don't really have very much, especially after posting bail—"

"Which you will get back, particularly when the charges are dropped," Mountain noted.

"Sure, in theory," she agreed, "but I guess I don't really trust the system enough to believe that I'll get it all back."

"Oh, I wouldn't worry about that," Aiden stated, his tone grim. "We'll make a big public stink about everybody who had something to do with your case—to the point that they'll be more than happy to give you every penny back, just so you didn't have a leg to stand on when it came down to filing complaints against the police department."

She smiled. "It's nice having somebody here to help me out, … to support me and to believe in me."

"You just forget about your parents. They can handle their own problems," Mountain said. "As you can tell, there's an awful lot of unhappiness there."

She nodded and looked down at the folders. "It's hard to

get the picture of that man and my father out of my mind."

"You just dump it," he advised. "Your father is entitled to live life as he wants, but he's not entitled to hurt anyone."

"He has never hurt me," she replied, "well, only emotionally and verbally, but no more since I cut him out of my life."

"And that's good that you finally cut him out," Mountain snapped, "because he is an asshole."

Hard to argue that because it was true.

Aiden hopped up, grabbed his keys, looked over at Mountain and Toby, and asked, "Are you coming?"

"Hell yes." She smiled. "You won't keep me away from this one."

Mountain nodded. "Absolutely. Never know when this will blow up, get even worse for Toby."

"We've got to get Toby out of this murder rap, safe and sound, and have the charges dropped," Aiden said, staring at Toby as he spoke. "But Mountain and I both know you won't have a life, Toby, particularly here, if we don't get the killer." He looked at her and nodded. "Let's go."

Mountain took care of transferring the files and the gun into the vehicle.

Aiden wrapped an arm around her shoulders and walked out with her, nuzzling her neck for the first time.

"Is that just for appearances?" she asked.

"In what way?" he asked, a hint of laughter in his voice.

"Ah, so you think somebody out here will be watching this?"

"I'll always assume somebody's watching you," he confirmed, with a smile. "The trick is to not let anybody else know that you know that."

She shook her head. "Everything is some sort of joke to

you."

"None of this is a joke." He turned her face to look at him. "But I want people to know that you aren't alone and that you do have friends, who will help to look after you."

"And I appreciate that," she replied. "It never occurred to me how alone anybody could feel, until something like this happens, and it's like all the rats desert the ship."

"That's another reason why I was wondering if you were really dedicated to staying here," he added, "because a whole wide world is out there. You wouldn't have to be looking at those stares from everybody who may be wondering if you really did kill your husband."

"God, they will be saying and thinking that, won't they?"

"Probably for quite a while. At least until the court case, whenever we get this guy who is killing these people."

"And yet my cousin has to leave soon."

"Mountain has to leave as soon as he gets the call. But I'm not sure when that'll be just yet, and we won't have a whole lot of notice."

"And then you'll leave too, won't you?" An odd tone filled her voice.

They were almost at the vehicle. With Mountain loading the boxes, Aiden turned her in his arms and said, "I'm here for as long as I'm needed."

"And then you'll leave," she said, with a definitive nod. "Got it."

He looked at her with a quirk of his lips and added, "Unless something keeps me here."

Her eyes widened. "Oh, gee, I wonder what that would be."

"A friend," he replied, tossing her another cheeky grin.

"Yeah. Like I have so many of those."

"You have me," he said. "You have your cousin."

She nodded. "And I can't mistake that because you guys have been a godsend so far. I can't even imagine what would have happened if we hadn't found all that blackmail stuff."

"None of it is for sure yet either, remember? And, if anybody is watching, let's give them a real good snapshot moment."

He drew her into his arms unprotestingly and kissed her gently at first, but her reaction surprised him. And when she suddenly threw her arms around his neck, he was caught by the surge of passion that overtook them both. When he finally pulled back, he was breathing hard. He stared down at her. "Jesus, I wasn't expecting that."

"Oh, you mean, it's just you who gets to play make believe?" she teased, batting her eyes at him. Appearing completely unconcerned, she walked over to the vehicle and got in the front passenger's side.

He stared at her and shook his head. "If that was acting, you're a hell of an actress."

"I am," she stated, with a broad smile.

At that, Mountain chuckled. "You guys, I keep telling you that you're perfect together."

"You never once told me that," she protested.

"I've been telling him, but he has this thing about you're a part of my family and that he's on a mission so …"

"All he's been doing is pushing you as being a great choice," she told Aiden, then added an eye roll. "It's a little bit hard to handle, actually."

"Why?" Aiden asked. "I am a good choice. But what are we choosing me for?"

"She shouldn't be alone anymore," Mountain declared

in a strong voice.

"Jeez, now don't you get started on it," she complained. "All my girlfriends at work have been telling me that I need to hook up with somebody. And they didn't even know about my relationship with Moscow."

"Well, you certainly wouldn't feel comfortable telling them about him, would you?" Aiden asked.

"No," she agreed, "yet he was always around. Somehow they were jealous that I could nab him. They just didn't understand that there was no nabbing. I was already caught. All I was trying to do was get free of that damn hook."

"Well, you're free now."

"And the trouble with that is," she added in a gloomy voice, "that's exactly why everybody thinks I killed him."

Aiden climbed into the driver's seat, while Mountain took the back seat. When they got to the detective's address, Aiden looked up at it and said, "Well, here goes nothing."

"I think we should all go in," she suggested.

"Yeah, I agree," Aiden said, "but first I need to ensure he's here, since I didn't call ahead." And he hopped out, walked up to the house and knocked, while Mountain and Toby watched him.

# CHAPTER 10

TOBY WATCHED AS Aiden walked up to the front door, and an older man stepped out, gray-haired, almost a buzz cut, as if he was heavy-duty military. They spoke for a moment, and then Aiden waved them to come up. Almost immediately, Mountain grabbed the two big boxes that they had filled with the blackmail files, and she grabbed several of the other bags of evidence, like the gun and some research in pertinent parties, and headed to the front door. The stranger saw the boxes and the bags, shook his head, and asked, "I won't like this, will I?"

"You obviously knew we were coming," Toby noted.

"Sure." He nodded. "Let's go into my office."

They walked past an older woman, sitting serenely with a cup of tea. Aiden nodded. "Thank you, ma'am. So sorry for disturbing you this morning."

She just inclined her head. "When trouble comes calling, young man," she murmured, "it doesn't give any warning, or he'd have time of day or peace of mind." With that cryptic tone, she lifted her cup and ignored them.

Back in his office, the detective looked at the boxes and raised his eyebrows, waiting.

Aiden began, "You're familiar with the case of the six murdered men, found stabbed to death and in the Dumpsters?"

"Yes," he said, crossing his arms, as he sat back in his big leather chair. "And I understand it has to do with you, young lady."

She nodded. "I've been charged with murdering my husband, Moscow," she replied, stumbling over the word. The detective's gaze narrowed on her face. "I didn't do it, but, when we were at his apartment, cleaning out his place," she added, "we found all kinds of files that indicate a blackmail scheme."

At that, his feet hit the floor, and he stared at the boxes. "All that is blackmail files?" Both men nodded. "Good God. And why me?"

"Because I asked for somebody who was honest," Aiden stated.

He winced at that. "Are there names in there that I won't like seeing?"

"Yep, absolutely," Aiden confirmed, "and you can start with the DA."

His breath hissed out in a long slow release. "We have had some suspicions that he's not on the up-and-up already," he replied, "but this? This will make life a little difficult."

"Not only a little difficult. A lot difficult. Also cops are listed in here," Aiden added, tapping the topmost box. "The other thing to note is that Toby's father is in here too as a blackmail victim," Aiden shared. "On the other hand, absolutely no love is lost between her and her family or her cousin Mountain and his family. Therefore, that is another motive that the cops or her family would mention, depending on which way you want to look at this."

The detective nodded his head slowly. "Do you think that this blackmail scheme has something to do with Moscow's murder?"

She shrugged. "It's certainly much more likely than me killing him. I can't even lift that man and certainly couldn't have thrown his body into a Dumpster."

The detective assessed her slim build and nodded. "I believe the current theory is that you have an accomplice," he noted, turning to look at Aiden.

"Well, you can check," Aiden suggested, "and preferably with my boss first." He placed a business card on the detective's desk. "But I have alibis for every night that those six men were murdered."

The detective picked up the card and read it. "I probably don't need to check this, do I?"

"Only if it makes you feel better," Aiden replied. "Mountain is in the same boat." Mountain placed his card on the desk in front of the detective too.

Toby wished she could see what the cards revealed because the detective immediately put them both in his shirt pocket.

"So, with that out of the way, what else have you got for me?"

"Little black book, bank accounts, all kinds of related research data, plus a gun, keys to safe deposit, a storage unit we have someone checking out," Aiden noted. "But we have absolutely no idea—outside of the fact that these people were being blackmailed—what happened to the money, where the money went, even if any blackmail money was paid, or anything like that," he shared. "Her husband was also a known gambler and was well-known for being lucky."

"So he had a lot of cash floating around?"

She nodded. "Yes."

"And why is it that you mentioned 'his apartment'? Have you recently been married?"

"As you probably know," she told him, "we were married just before he was killed."

"And you told the police that it wasn't a happy marriage and that you didn't want to marry him but you did anyway."

She took a deep breath, looked over at Aiden.

"What you need to understand is the rest of the story, which she hasn't told the police," Aiden stated.

The detective pulled out a tape recorder and placed it on his desk. "Then it's time you told someone." He motioned at the chairs and said, "Sit."

She sat down and then nervously started telling him about her high school days, the breakup, the threats, Moscow's abuse of his sister, and then finally Moscow beating her up, pointing a gun at her, and forcing her to marry him to keep his sister safe. At that, the detective stared at her, his eyes turning dark. "Sounds like quite an upstanding citizen."

"He was a bastard," she stated bitterly. "And I'm pretty sure his father is applying a lot of pressure to the cops to make sure that I am incarcerated for his son's death. But I swear to you that I had nothing to do with it."

"And of course you have proof of the beating?" the detective asked.

She gave a slight smile. "Why is it that everybody always wants proof of that?"

"That's because it's physical proof."

She pulled up her phone, brought up the picture that Annabel had sent her, and held it up for him.

He looked at it and winced.

She nodded. "He didn't break anything that I know of. For all I know, a couple cracked ribs have since healed. I didn't go to the hospital, so I don't know. Believe me. He didn't do it again, but he also agreed to my terms on the marriage."

"And did you believe him?"

"I did at the time, but, as these two have convinced me, it wouldn't have lasted."

"No, it wouldn't. Now, when you got in an abusive relationship, he made you legally his in his mind to do what he wished, so he would just torment you for however long he wanted to play with you, just like he did with his sister. What kind of shape is his sister in?"

Toby shook her head. "She still calls me in torment, and she's quite psychologically damaged by it all."

"Right," the detective agreed. "And, of course, we have absolutely no medical evidence of that either."

"No," Toby confirmed, "nor do I have any proof of the damage he did to her. Except I've seen her decline, and I've talked to her through many nightmares."

"And that's something we have yet to do," Aiden noted. "We'll speak with Michelle after this."

Toby nodded. "I just don't want her even more upset."

"And will the presence of these two men upset her?" the detective asked.

"It's possible. But she's definitely not the same person she used to be."

He nodded. "So Moscow liked to abuse women and children—vulnerable members of society?"

"Yes," she stated, "but he was blackmailing big names in town."

"Right. But that was probably done anonymously, until somebody must have found out and possibly started this murder spree."

"That's what we're assuming. Of course we have no way

to know for sure right now," Aiden added.

"Right. We'll have to follow up on all this." The detective faced Toby and asked, "What is it you want from me?"

"I want to clear my name. I want the truth," she replied, "and I definitely don't trust the cops who are working on my case."

The detective nodded. "I'll get a major shuffle of the people assigned to the case. I'll have to check the blackmail files you brought me to make sure that they're not in any of those." At that, his lips twitched. He looked over at Aiden. "Unless you want to tell me."

"One is. One isn't." At that, Toby turned and stared at him. He shrugged. "You didn't ask."

"I didn't ask, so you didn't just tell me?"

"It seemed like the safest bet at the time."

She just shook her head. "No wonder they didn't give a crap about getting me a fair shake. No wonder those fake cops wanted inside Moscow's apartment. They're probably afraid of what I'll do with all this information."

"And you have the capacity to do all kinds of things," said the detective in front of her. "And I presume you have copies of all this?"

Aiden nodded. "We do," he confirmed cheerfully.

The detective smiled. "So, if I don't follow through, you have another recourse."

"I know you'll follow through," Aiden stated. "But, should any of these weasels squeak away, we have the ability to make their lives miserable, once it's public knowledge what they're up to. Marriages will dissolve. Divorces will spike, and there'll be a lot more resignations and lawsuits happening," he declared.

At that, the detective nodded. "It will be quite a mess."

"And yet it's not our fault," Toby declared defiantly. "I didn't do anything to deserve this."

"No, and you've been a long time trying to get out of this domestic abuse by both father and son," the detective noted. "So let's hope that, once I take all this in and go above the DA," he said, rubbing his temples, "we can put a stop to that and to the murder charges."

"And I presume you can get an appointment with the DOJ?" Aiden asked.

"Yes." The detective nodded. "Like I said, there's already been talk about the DA."

"Good," Toby said. "This is the ammo you need then. The gun alone may incriminate Moscow in even more shady acts."

"It all might, indeed. I'll check for the report. Somehow I doubt it will be that easy." The detective stared down at the boxes and the bags of paperwork, like it would bite him. "It also won't be a fun trip."

"Nothing about this is a fun trip," Toby admitted, "particularly for me. I just want a new beginning."

"Are you planning on staying in town?"

"No," she replied immediately. "I do hate to leave Michelle behind. However, as these men have just pointed out to me, my life will never be the same here, even if I am cleared."

The detective nodded. "Your husband was a blackmailer, and you were his wife, even if just for a short period of time. Some people will always wonder," he murmured, "and, for that, I'm sorry."

"Me too," she agreed.

"But it is what it is."

She laughed. "That sounds like my father."

"And how would your father handle all this?"

"He refuses to stand by me, and he won't handle any of this," she stated. "And you'll find him in the blackmail files for having a gay romance. Then he'll just blame me even more."

He nodded. "Sorry, but it is what happens a lot of the time."

"I know," she said, "and that's frustrating, but there's nothing I can do about it. He made his choices, and he'll have to pay for them."

"And yet there isn't any reason why he couldn't have a relationship that he's chosen, is there?" the detective asked her.

"No, except that he's married," she stated. "And you have to understand that my mother is all about appearances. It will be a very ugly divorce."

He nodded. "I don't think there is such a thing as a pleasant divorce."

"Maybe not, but this one will take the cake."

"Got it. Where are you guys off to now?"

Toby looked over at Aiden. "I'll take them to see Michelle. And then we'll go from there."

"Good. Will you get in my way?" the detective asked the men, looking at Aiden and then at Mountain.

"Not if you don't get in our way," Mountain vowed, before Aiden could speak.

At that, the detective's gaze narrowed.

"We need to find out who's behind all these murders," Aiden explained. "Otherwise Toby will never really be free. You can drop the charges, but, now that she has been charged, you know how almost everybody'll think that it was her."

Again the detective nodded. "That is a problem when the department charges people without thinking about it, without a shred of evidence. Lives are altered forever."

"You can say that again," Toby said. "I'll probably end up leaving the state."

"Well, don't leave now," he warned her. "Let us get to the bottom of this first."

"I'm under bond and will not default. I also don't have any intention of leaving today or tomorrow," she replied. "But after that bond is released? Well, I don't know."

The detective turned toward Aiden. "You know perfectly well that she needs to stay until this is done."

"I know that," Aiden agreed. "It's been a pretty rough ride on her already. So we'll spend the day following clues, seeing what we can find, and go from there."

"And what about the other murders?" the detective asked, now looking over at her. "Do you have any idea who's involved?"

She immediately shook her head. "No. All six men, including Moscow, won a lot of money at my table," she shared. "I think the cops' prevailing theory is that I let these six guys win, and then I went to get my share of their earnings. Supposedly, when they wouldn't share, I killed them and took all the money." Toby frowned. "From what we've read in the police reports, none of the dead men were found with any money on them, but you also know that any number of people gamble at a casino in any given day, and so there's thousands of faces and heads to track through their casinos' camera software. So you'll see that any number of other people could have found out that these six men just won big. When the big winners went outside the casino, they became victims of greed."

"It's not all that uncommon," the detective noted. "It's just happening so fast that no really good answer explains it."

"Well, there is one," she stated. "I just don't know what it is." As she stood up, Toby added, "Thank you for this. At least, I thank you."

Aiden gave the detective a fat smile. "Hey, you're it, so do a good job."

"*Or else*, right?" the detective teased.

"No. No threats," Aiden said. "You were given the highest recommendation possible for this," he noted, "so I trust that you'll do the best job you can."

"Oh, great," the detective said, with a wry smile. "No pressure."

"There's always pressure in life," Aiden noted, with a laugh. And, with that, he headed out to the front door. As soon as he stepped outside, he looked over at Toby and said, "You did well back there."

"I don't feel like it. Kind of feels very much like I'm failing something majorly."

"Let's go see your sister-in-law," Aiden said, changing the subject and moving forward.

At that, she stopped, looked at him, and said, "Wow. She really is my sister-in-law, isn't she?"

"You really disassociated from all of it, didn't you?" Mountain asked.

"Sure," she murmured. "I mean, understandably so."

"Absolutely," he agreed. "It's just odd to see you always argue about the naming of things, the titles, and the labels."

"That's because I wasn't even married but a few days," she muttered.

"And somebody did you a hell of a favor."

She nodded. "I know that. I really do. The trouble is, I

also know that whoever did that probably has no clue what kind of trouble they put me into."

"Or, if they did, it was deliberate," Aiden pointed out.

"And I can see that maybe with Moscow. However," she argued, "when you think about it, why take out him *and* the other five? Or can there be two different killers?"

"I was wondering about that. Your husband was what? The third murder?"

She nodded. "Yes, third. Well, per the estimated time of death, pending the coroner's report, but not in the order of dead bodies found."

Aiden nodded. "So, it's pretty easy to kill them and then just toss their bodies in a Dumpster. I mean, all they have in common regarding their deaths are the same manner of killing—a knife—and their bodies found in Dumpsters in the same general location." Then he asked for directions on how to get to Michelle's group home.

AS SOON AS they pulled up at the large institutional-looking home, he studied it from the vehicle and asked, "So who all lives here?"

"Special needs individuals who can handle independent living with some assistance," Toby replied. "Michelle can live just fine on her own, but, of course, making some decisions and looking after the house and whatnot are difficult for her. She doesn't cook very well and is not very capable in the kitchen. She's great at helping but not in making a whole meal, so this is kind of like a care home or a halfway house environment."

"So everybody here is dealing with some sort of mental

disability?"

"Yes." Toby nodded. "I think the bulk of them are chromosome-type diseases, like Down syndrome, but I can't be sure. I just know Michelle has that."

"She's been diagnosed as having Down syndrome?"

"Yes," she murmured. "Although I know that Moscow and his father would never acknowledge it."

"Well, it doesn't matter if you acknowledge it or not," Aiden said. "It would make it a lot easier on Michelle if people did understand just what the problem was."

"Exactly," Toby agreed, "and honestly Michelle and I have been close for a long time. I know that she's still not sleeping well, but I haven't seen her since her brother's death."

"Why?"

"Because I didn't know what to say to her," she admitted. "Yet I have talked to her by phone. I even told her Moscow was dead. I know somebody at the home already explained that to her."

"Right. And who would that be?"

"Her assigned matron maybe?" she replied, with a shrug. They got out, walked up to the front door, and entered without anybody stopping them.

"So, really no security in a place like this," Aiden noted, with a quick glance at Mountain, who frowned.

"No, not at all," Toby said. "Should there be?"

Aiden just shrugged. "Hard for me to say yet," he murmured. "It's really close to everything, isn't it?"

"It is. The residents often walk around town together. They go shopping together," she said, "or, at least, they go out in groups of two, three, or four."

"Right. So they have overseers, like the matron you mentioned, like a den mother?" Aiden asked.

"Yes," Toby confirmed, smiling at him.

"So the kids must really love it."

"Most of them aren't kids anymore, but, yes, that's exactly how they feel about it. I'm sure they have a lot more freedom—their space away from family—that can be both good and bad."

Aiden didn't say much as they walked deeper inside, and she headed toward the main common room. As she looked around, a couple people stood nearby, talking. One lifted a hand and waved at her with a big smile. She waved back immediately. She walked over to the boy who had waved at her. "Any idea where Michelle is?"

"In room," he said, his voice husky and slightly off. "She's in her room."

"Good," Toby said. "We'll go find her there." Everybody watched as they left.

"Kind of an odd feel to the place," Aiden noted.

"Well, it has always been pretty friendly to me," Toby stated, "so I don't know about *off*. Just feels very much like I am in another home. I've seen her in a couple different ones. I know that this one has been the happiest of them."

"Right," Aiden noted.

As they got to Michelle's room on the second floor, Toby knocked, and there was no answer. She frowned. "I wonder if she's sleeping." She poked her head gently around the door and whispered, "Michelle, you awake?" They heard some movement inside. She looked back at the guys and said, "Just give me a minute." She walked inside and closed the door. Aiden and Mountain stood here in the hallway, watching as a few other people came and went.

Mountain whispered to Aiden, "I'm probably scaring

some people here. I'll go take a sweep around outside, maybe a block or two away. I'll meet up with you guys later." And he disappeared.

Now that Aiden was alone, still nobody stopped and asked him what he was doing, until another young man stopped and smiled at him.

"Michelle is nice," he said, motioning at the door to her room.

"Is she?" Aiden asked, with a quiet smile. "She's happy here, isn't she?"

The young man immediately nodded. "Yes, very happy. She doesn't want to leave," he stated, and his face suddenly got really serious, as if he thought that's why Aiden was here.

"We're not here to take her away," Aiden said immediately. "We're just visiting Michelle."

The other man's face cleared, and he nodded. "Good. She's happy here." And, with that, he went down the hallway a little bit but kept looking back at Aiden.

"Is there something you want to tell me?" Aiden asked the young man, before he'd gotten too far away.

He just shook his head. "No, she's happy here."

"Good. I'm glad to hear that she's happy here." Yet Aiden still had that sense that the young man wanted to say something more. Aiden just didn't know how to get him to open up. And why should he talk to him when obviously other people were all around who he could talk to who he knew better?

When the man returned to him, Aiden just waited and smiled. "Do you spend much time with her?"

He immediately nodded. "We help each other," he noted.

"In what way?" Aiden asked.

The other man shrugged. "We play games. We exercise," he said, and, with a proud smile, lifted up his T-shirt to show the muscles and the biceps bulging underneath.

"Wow," Aiden said, seriously impressed. "That's awesome."

The other man smiled. "Yeah, it's really good," he said, with that sense of almost childlike accomplishment, and yet this guy was an adult.

Aiden nodded. "It's not easy to make those kinds of gains at a gym."

"Not easy." The other man nodded. "I work hard."

"I'm sure you do, and you should be proud of your progress," Aiden added.

At that moment, an adult wearing a name tag walked down the hallway, saw Aiden, and frowned. "Hey," she called out.

Aiden held up a hand and motioned at the door in front of them. "I came with Toby to visit Michelle."

The worry on the woman's face cleared. "Is Toby in there?"

He nodded. "I gather Michelle isn't up yet."

"She's not having very good days," the woman explained. "I'm Ann, by the way. I'm one of the adults around this place," she explained.

At that, the young man shook his head. "I'm an adult."

"Yes, you are," she stated. She looked over at Aiden. "Michelle has not been having it easy these past few days."

"Because of her brother's death presumably."

"We'll see how Michelle is when she comes out today."

The door opened, and Toby stepped out, a smile on her face, which slowly disappeared when she saw Ann. "Hey, Ann." She motioned at Aiden. "He's with me."

"Good," she said. "How is Michelle?"

"I would ask you that," Toby told Ann. "She doesn't look like she's handling life very well right now."

"No," the den mother said. "I did mention it to the psychologist, who was here a few days ago," she shared. "But nobody is really sure how much of it is related to her brother's death."

"She's not doing very well," Toby stated. "I am quite concerned about her mental state."

Just then, the door opened, and Michelle stepped out into the hallway. Her eyes were red and puffy, as if she'd been crying a lot. As soon as she saw Aiden, she immediately stepped closer to Toby. Michelle had her arms wrapped around her chest, as if protecting herself, guarding herself from something.

Michelle never seemed to note the young man standing with Aiden. Maybe Aiden's presence was enough to distract her.

"It's okay, Michelle," Toby said, putting an arm around Michelle's shoulders. "This is Aiden, the friend I told you about."

She looked at Aiden with an intense scrutiny, and then, as if seeming to accept Toby at her word, Michelle nodded. "He friend."

"Yes, he's a friend," Toby reiterated.

At that, Michelle wiped her nose on her sleeve, like a two-year-old, and smiled at Aiden. "Hi."

He gave her the gentlest of smiles and replied, "Hi, Michelle. Nice to meet you."

She studied him for a long moment. "You know my brother?"

He shook his head. "No, I did not."

And then she said, "Good." And, with that, she turned to Toby. "Can we go eat?"

"Yes, absolutely." She turned and looked at Ann, who still stood with them. "Has she had any food lately?"

Ann immediately shook her head. "She didn't show up for breakfast." She looked at Michelle and said, "Stick to cereal or toast, okay?"

Michelle nodded and headed to the kitchen, and everybody else had to keep up.

He grabbed Toby's hand. "How is she?"

"Not good," she said. "I think she's been crying nonstop."

"And do we know why?"

"No, we don't, and it could take a while to figure it out." She sighed heavily. "Some days are good, and then some days aren't good."

At that, the young man—who had stuck with them as a group—said, "No good days now."

"And why isn't she having good days now?" Toby asked him, carefully studying his features, as if that would tell her something. Toby asked the young man, "Is it because of her brother?"

The man nodded. "Bad man," he said, "very bad man."

"Yes, he was," Toby agreed immediately, "but he's dead."

The young man nodded. "Yes, dead, … dead. And that's a good thing."

She didn't want to reiterate that point, so she stayed quiet. She asked him, "When did Michelle eat last?"

Michelle turned to Toby, a cross look on her face. "I ate dinner."

"Good," Toby said in a bright tone. "I'm glad you're

eating, even though you're upset."

"I like eating," Michelle stated. "I don't like my brother." And such pain filled her voice that Aiden could hardly hold back his wince.

*What kind of an asshole would torment somebody like this?* And yet he knew it wasn't just about Michelle's brother. Unfortunately people abused innocent people all the time. Just broke his heart though. As they headed into the kitchen, he stayed slightly back and behind. The young man stayed behind too. As Aiden leaned against the doorjamb and crossed his arms over his chest, he noted with a twinge of amusement as the young man did the same thing. Aiden caught the young man studying Aiden, and he gave a nod of approval. Almost instinctively the young man straightened his shoulders. "What's your name?" Aiden asked.

"Rick," he replied.

"Good. So, Rick, are you a good friend of Michelle's?"

Rick nodded. "I help her lots. I'm strong. I can do things."

"I'm glad to hear that," Aiden said. "What kind of things?" he asked in a hesitant voice.

At that moment, an argument erupted between Michelle and Ann. "I don't want that cereal," she argued, staring at Ann in horror. "I want my cereal."

"We're out, remember?" Ann said. "You were responsible for putting it on the shopping list. It didn't go on the list, and it didn't get picked up."

Aiden knew a crisis was about to happen. He looked over at Toby to see her trying to figure out a way to handle it. He nudged her gently. "Are we allowed to take her out?"

She nodded and stepped forward. "And how about we take her, get her outside for a little bit, maybe head down to the pancake place?"

At that, Michelle turned and looked at her in hope. "I have no cereal," she stated.

"And you know why," Ann said in a firm voice.

"Maybe we can resolve this problem just because we're here now, today," Toby said gently. "We need coffee and maybe some lunch."

"Lunch," Michelle agreed, nodding her head. "Let's go for lunch." She looked back and asked, "Rick come too?"

And that was a first apparently because Toby asked her, "You want Rick to come for lunch?"

She nodded. "Rick my friend," she said proudly.

Toby turned toward Rick, standing there beside Aiden, both of them in identical poses, and her lips twitched. She looked at Aiden and asked, "Are you okay with that?"

He immediately nodded. "Sure, why not?" he said, and they all walked back to the vehicle, with the two of them chattering away on a million things that seemed completely unrelated to what was going on. Aiden quickly sent a text to Mountain, updating him. Mountain sent a reply that he'd find his own way back home.

As the four of them got in the vehicle, Aiden looked over at Toby. "Any progress?"

She shook her head. "No, but any mention is likely to set her off."

"Right," he said, realizing just how much that could be an issue if they were heading to a restaurant.

Toby shrugged. "You know there are good days and bad days."

"And is this a good day or a bad day?"

She smiled. "You know what? I'm tempted to say it's a bad day, but I'm not sure—compared to what I'm hearing from the others. Seems maybe it's a good day because her other days have been so rough."

"And that would be tough if she didn't understand that he's gone. That alone might help."

"It might help a lot," Toby agreed, "but somehow I have to get that through to her."

Aiden nodded, not sure how to work it either.

# CHAPTER 11

L UNCH PROCEEDED AT a decent pace, with everybody in a bright mood, although the overarching problem remained that Toby was trying to figure out.

At one point, Rick mentioned Moscow. "Bad man gone. He won't hurt you no more." Almost immediately Michelle nodded and reached over and held his hand.

Toby had no idea how relationships were handled in homes for special needs individuals like this. Were they on birth control? Were they told about the birds and the bees? Toby was not sure she wanted to get into all that. Not sure she could, due to HIPAA and other privacy laws. However, it was obvious that the two of them were very close. She'd have to talk to Ann about it, yet she didn't want to cause any more upset for her sister-in-law's peace and happiness. Toby faced Michelle. "And you do understand Moscow's gone, right?"

She nodded. "He won't hurt me anymore."

"No. That's quite true," Toby agreed. Pancakes were delivered all around, and Michelle and Rick dove in as if they hadn't eaten in weeks.

Toby noted the surprise on Aiden's face. She smiled. "It's really normal," she noted. He just closed his mouth and didn't say anything, and she appreciated that. He seemed to understand very well that there was a time to talk and a time not to. She'd always found dealing with Michelle to be one of judging moods more than timing. When Toby considered the issue of Moscow's death, she wondered if it was important who told the two or not, and then realized it really didn't matter, as long as Michelle understood.

At that point Michelle patted Toby's hand and added, "He won't hurt you anymore either."

Startled, Toby replied, "That's right. I didn't realize you knew that he'd hurt me."

Michelle nodded. "He hurts everyone."

"Unfortunately that's probably quite true," Toby admitted.

"It's just very sad. Very sad," her sister-in-law replied, but such cheerfulness filled her voice that it seemed to Toby as if there wasn't any real recognition of what *sad* meant.

When her sister-in-law finished all her pancakes on her plate, Toby asked, "Now how do you feel?"

"Better, not so hungry." She looked over at Rick. "Rick is feeling better too."

"Good," Toby stated. "How come you guys had such a big appetite?"

"Exercise," Michelle said immediately.

"Right. You guys working out?" Toby asked.

Michelle nodded. "He's teaching me self-defense." That brought the conversation to a complete close.

Toby took in a slow breath. "We're back to the fact that your brother is dead," she murmured. "Remember?"

"I know," Michelle confirmed. "I know." Then she leaned forward and whispered, "I'm not supposed to tell anyone, so you're the only one we can tell."

"Tell me what?" Toby asked.

Her sister-in-law leaned closer, looked at Rick, who had

a big grin on his face, and she whispered, "We killed him."

The blood in Toby's veins froze.

AIDEN DIDN'T KNOW how either of them got out of the restaurant and got their two charges back to the home while maintaining any kind of sanity. Every time they tried to ask them questions, both of them buttoned up, as if they had some major secrets still left to share. For all of Toby's attempts, she couldn't get anything out of them either. When they finally walked back to the vehicle after delivering the couple to their group home, Aiden and Toby just sat there.

Toby whispered, "Dear God."

"I know," he agreed. "I've been thinking about the consequences of all that."

She stared at him and whispered, "Oh my God."

He nodded. "Let's go home." They slowly drove back to her place, even though it was not very far.

"Before we go home," Toby suggested, "let's go back to where Moscow's body was found."

Aiden shook his head. "I don't even think we need to physically go there. We need to bring it up on a map."

She nodded. "That Dumpster's not very far away from them at the home, is it?"

"No, it's not," he confirmed. "Depending on the route they took, based on a map, if they went all the way around the block, the Dumpster would be a couple blocks away. However, if this young man—who's been working out and has put on a fair bit of muscle—had cut across the home's backyard, they could have made the trip shorter. Rick may have lifted Moscow's body up and over the fence around the home. So it wouldn't have been hard to dump Moscow into the Dumpster on the other side."

"That's all they had to do, isn't it? Go out the back door, out the back alley, and that is the one and only Dumpster on the next street over. And Michelle had talked about the garbage earlier," Toby noted. "I just didn't make any kind of nefarious connection."

"Are you saying that we believe this could have happened?" Aiden asked her, as he pulled up in front of her place.

She got out and walked around the vehicle to stand beside him. "I can't even begin to imagine, except for the fact that I know how traumatized Michelle was."

As they got into her house, Mountain looked up at them and immediately frowned. "Okay, so something has happened."

Toby plunked herself down on the nearest chair. "Something has definitely happened, but the ramifications are horrific." And she told her cousin what the couple had said at lunch.

Mountain whistled. "Good God. And do you really think she and Rick did this?"

"I don't know," Toby replied, bewildered. "Is it possible? Absolutely. Did Michelle have a motive? Absolutely. Would she have done it cognitively, understanding what she did? She certainly would have understood that she was getting rid of a threat or trying to stop him. Would she have understood the consequences? No, of course not." Toby shook her head. "But, I mean, what am I supposed to do with this information?"

Mountain stated, "First off, this is a theory, unless you

have any proof—other than Michelle's statement?"

Toby shook her head, mute, in shock.

They all sat here quietly, and Aiden suggested, "We need to contact the detective."

"And yet we don't know anything on a concrete evidentiary level," Mountain noted.

Toby nodded. "We know it's *possible* they could have done it, in the sense that Moscow was found in a Dumpster not very far away from their group home. And we do know that the young man Rick has been working out and is much stronger than we probably would have considered, prior to going there. But that—"

"I know," Aiden agreed. "The *buts* really get us on this. … I wish we had some idea of what happened to the other men who were murdered."

"Well, I might help you there," Mountain said. "I did get a phone call from the same detective who you'll want to talk to about this Michelle comment. The cops found another body last night."

She stared at her cousin. "I have an alibi this time."

He nodded. "You do have an alibi, and that is pretty huge."

"But not huge enough?" she asked sadly. "Maybe the cops will drop the charges?"

"The detective has asked that you go down and meet your lawyer at the police station. They are prepared to drop all charges."

Toby leaned back and closed her eyes. "Thank God." After a moment, she sat up, eyes wide open. "And I have to sign some forms, I presume?"

He nodded. "Yes."

"And I never got my lawyer signed up."

"He made a couple phone calls on your behalf. I don't know if he'll charge you for that service or not," Mountain noted, "but the bottom line is, you're free and clear."

"And that's huge too," she stated, letting out a big sigh of relief. "So I guess that's a bigger bottom line than anything so far yet."

Aiden smiled at her. "I don't know about that," he added, "but let's take it one step at a time."

It didn't take long to get to the station, to get confirmation that all charges had been dropped, and to sign any related forms. As she walked outside, she murmured, "And now you realize Moscow's father will be after blood."

"Yeah, and that's quite possible," Aiden admitted. "So we have another problem there, and Michelle's also his daughter, correct?"

"Stepdaughter," she murmured, "but, yes, family, definitely family. I don't even want to think about what might happen to her."

"I'm not sure very much can happen at all without evidence," Aiden noted, "and that would be a reason to have a *very* good lawyer appointed for Michelle."

Toby stared at him. "How do we prove if Michelle and Rick did it or not?"

"Security cameras?"

"Maybe." Toby frowned. "The home should have them."

"I don't know. I'm sure there are all kinds of rules and regulations regarding personal privacy, plus any related HIPAA rules too."

"I'm sure there are," she agreed.

"Let me look into it. I'll get Corbin on it." And, with that, Aiden sent Corbin a text message, asking if any security cameras were at the group home and if they could access those feeds. Almost immediately Aiden got a response back saying there weren't any.

Damn. Of course not. Likely an infringement of their privacy. Damn.

# CHAPTER 12

TOBY MADE DINNER for everyone but almost in an automatic robotic mode. Steak and corn on the cob and a big green salad should work for these guys. When they sat down to eat, she said, "One thing gets me."

Aiden looked over at her. "What?"

"Just how proud they were," she murmured. "Like they'd solved the problem, and it wasn't even that they got away with it because I don't think they have any understanding of *getting away with something*. Just that they dealt with Moscow's abuse and that he wouldn't ever bother Michelle again. … Did the coroner confirm how Moscow died?" she asked.

"Not sure we have the death certificates back on any of these murders. The police reports state Moscow was stabbed, just like the others." Aiden hesitated. "And why would Rick and Michelle do that?" he asked. "That can't be."

She stared at him. "Meaning?"

"There would have been blood at the crime scene."

She frowned at that. "No, you're right. And I can't see them stabbing somebody in the group home and not having anybody else notice."

"No, I don't think that could happen at all. Unless, of course, Rick was outside with Michelle or in another location."

"Did we ever get details of the last time Moscow visited her?" Mountain asked.

"No, not from Michelle or Rick anyway. And they wouldn't talk to us—they are still acting all *mum's the word*," she said, with a shudder. "I can't even imagine what to do about it," she muttered. "I mean, I was charged with Moscow's murder, and, of course, now the cops have dropped all the charges, but … what if me being safe and clear just means putting Michelle away? I don't think I can do that."

At that, Aiden put down his knife and fork, looked at her, and declared, "You won't take a fall for something like this."

"I don't know what the courts would do in this case," she muttered. "Michelle was traumatized, beaten, and horribly abused by her brother."

"Are you willing to testify to that fact?"

"Absolutely," she murmured, "and I have a lot of phone calls to the cops to back that up. Plus the group home knows perfectly well that Michelle was traumatized. Unfortunately nobody really believed who was responsible."

"But you do."

"Yes," she stated. "I do. But the authorities could still lock her up because she can't do this to the next person who upsets her."

At that, they all went silent.

"And she may never ever do it again," she muttered sadly. "Yet I don't know that for sure." She knew it would take her a while to work through this. "Still, we need to tell somebody."

"We also need to confirm that this is what happened," her cousin reminded her. "Just think about what it is that we're saying, and yet we have no proof."

"Proof of what? There are no video cameras in the home," she wailed.

Aiden added, "Obviously we don't think the stabbing scenario works within the group home setting. Rick's and Michelle's clothing would have been covered in blood. That would not be something they could hide."

Toby nodded. "And I haven't looked at her laundry. I think they do their own laundry there. … Originally they do it under supervision, but, once they know how to do it, then they're left to their own devices, with somebody just checking to make sure that laundry is done on a regular basis."

"So would her clothing on that day have already been washed?" Aiden asked her.

"Moscow died some two weeks ago," she replied, "so, in theory, yes."

"What are the chances that she just hid the clothes or that she threw them away?" Aiden suggested alternatively.

"I don't know," she replied, still stunned at just the logistics of what those two may have pulled off. "However, they could have dumped their clothes in the same Dumpster, along with Moscow."

"And, if the cops are doing their jobs, any bloody clothing found in the Dumpster next to Moscow's dead body is immediately suspect. They should have run DNA on those, if found." He paused. "Remember. They won't get away with anything," he noted gently.

"But getting away with something wasn't their goal," she murmured. "I think it was to just stop the abuse. At the time of his death, if he was doing something to her that he shouldn't be doing, then it would make a lot more sense."

Aiden hesitated and considered Toby for a moment. "I

know this is not something you want to think about, but did Moscow ever sexually assault Michelle?"

"I don't know," Toby said. "I really don't know. I often wondered, and she refused to even have conversations in that direction. She doesn't seem to want to discuss something like sex at all. It's hard for me to even know what her cognitive awareness is of the sex act."

"Right," Aiden agreed. "All kinds of different problems are here, aren't there?"

"There are so many of them," Toby murmured. "Would Moscow have raped her? I won't say no. He was an absolute bastard. He probably would have done it just to prove his control over her."

"In which case," Aiden added, "if she was being raped, and that's when killing Moscow happened, it would be self-defense. However, from what I understand of the laws, if they decided to do this too long afterward or when they happen to see him next, it muddies the water."

"I don't understand how that could have happened in the group home," she stated. "And any rape scene doesn't seem to work if Michelle and Rick were walking outside and ran into Moscow."

"Just theories so far," Aiden shrugged, but doubt filled his voice.

"It all seems so far-fetched," Toby said.

Aiden nodded. "You have to talk to her again." She frowned. "You know I'm right," he murmured.

"Maybe." She pinched the bridge of her nose. "But what am I supposed to do? Ask Michelle, *So, when you killed your brother, did you just casually think about it or did you plan this in advance?* I mean, how will I even get my intent across?"

"Maybe you need to talk to a specialist."

"I don't know." She buried her face in her hands. After a moment, she sat up and sighed. "I can't send her off to a life of imprisonment, if she and Rick killed Moscow. This poor woman has already suffered so much at the hands of her brother."

"And I hear you," Aiden agreed, "but I have absolutely no intention of letting you take the fall for something like that." She lifted her gaze to him. He shook his head. "I get it. It's a terrible thing. And, if ever a bastard deserved killing, it was Moscow. But that doesn't change the fact that you won't take the rap for Michelle. No reason for you to suffer for what somebody else does, especially after all you've suffered already."

Mountain added, "Plus you're getting way ahead of yourself, Toby. There's no evidence against Michelle. Slow down the guilt. Work the case logically."

She opened her mouth. Both guys shook their heads at her. She snapped it shut and then turned her glare at Aiden. "I didn't say I would take the rap for Michelle," she stated finally.

"You were thinking about it," he pointed out.

She continued to glare at Aiden.

Then her cousin started to chuckle. "I'm really glad you two found each other," he said. "I can go away happy."

At that, Aiden looked at him. "When are you leaving?"

"Not just yet." He frowned. "I'm still putting intel together, and logistically this isn't working out all that easily yet. So, even if I do have to run, I'll be a while getting my own act together on the other side."

"And you're being just more cryptic than ever," she stated, staring at her cousin. "The least you could do is explain some of this."

"I would if I could," he noted, "but, so far, it's still very unclear, even to me."

"I don't like to hear that," she replied. "I hope whatever you're heading into isn't dangerous."

He gave her a half smile and a snort. "Unfortunately I can't say that it isn't. When things go wrong in my world, things go very wrong."

"Has this got to do with your brother?" She narrowed her gaze at her cousin.

Aiden asked, "You have a brother?"

Mountain winced. "I do have a brother." He took a deep breath. "Yes, it does have to do with my brother."

"Oh, crap." She stared at Mountain in shock. "You know that's bad news."

"He's different now," he stated defensively.

She continued to stare at him. "He is?" she asked.

"You'll have to trust me on that."

She just shrugged.

"Okay. Well, I don't know anything about a brother," Aiden noted, looking from one to the other. "And it sounds like somebody needs to fill me in."

"His brother was another lovely family member who seemed to be just a mess all the time," she replied, without saying too much. "How did he possibly get his act together?" she asked, looking at Mountain.

"He went into the navy," he stated. "You'd be surprised just how much you get tuned up in there."

She looked over at Aiden for confirmation.

He immediately nodded. "Many a person has sent their troubled child into one of the services in order to get them cleaned up and turned around in life," he explained. "The military service has a well-known ability to do that, as long as you can conform. However, the service is pretty rough on those who can't."

"And it was rough on him for a long time," Mountain admitted, "but he ended up in a very good place." He looked over at Aiden and smiled. "Let's just say he took it like a duck takes to water."

"Ah, he ended up as a US Navy SEAL."

"He did, and then he was discharged and went into another black ops program."

"How many black ops programs are there?" she asked in astonishment, staring at them both. "That's what you guys are a part of, isn't it?"

Mountain nodded. "I am. For this job, yes."

"And I still don't understand that part," Aiden added.

"Because I need a machine behind me," he murmured. "And we have a big problem ahead, and having that machine behind me will be mandatory. However, my team has to be somebody I can trust, and the team must also be a black ops team, so that I can step out of the norm to get the job done."

She stared at him. "I don't like the sound of that," she said, her tone turning harsh.

He smiled. "Maybe not, and I don't know when, if, or how I'll be back."

She frowned. "You know how freaky that makes it sound, right?"

He nodded. "I know, but my brother is in trouble."

Her jaw opened, and once again she snapped it shut this time, with more force than was necessary. "And, as long as you figure you can do something, you'll go do it," she admitted, with a nod.

"And how do you feel about Michelle?" Mountain challenged.

She winced. "Just the same as you with your brother. God, what a mess."

⚓

"EXACTLY," MOUNTAIN AGREED, "and I'm trying to fix one mess before we get into the other one."

"I think it's too late for that," Toby noted, with an eye roll. "I mean, this one is going downhill very quickly."

"So the question is, *What do we do next?*" Mountain posed to both of them.

"I think we should go talk to the detective again," Aiden suggested, "and see if he has anything to follow up on."

"And that'll be on the now six other men but not necessarily my ex?"

"Exactly, but, at least per Michelle, your ex is the one case that's not the same."

"But didn't the cops say earlier that all the men were stabbed to death?"

"They may have told you that, but that doesn't mean that it's the truth. We need to double-check all those case files, plus read through the coroner's reports too, if they are available now."

She stared at him. "So the cops did that just to rattle me?"

Aiden nodded. "I think it was to make you think that it was all connected."

"Which is just an asshole move," she snapped.

"We already agree these cops were lacking a lot in integrity."

"Great," she muttered. "So now what do we do?"

"I think the answer is obvious. We need to take this new

information to somebody else."

"And what then? Do you think they'll go talk to Michelle?"

Aiden nodded. "That would be standard procedure. However, you know the authorities won't ever get a proper answer out of her, particularly if she's smart enough now to stay quiet."

"She isn't though," she admitted, staring at him. "And what am I supposed to do if I know the truth?"

"*Do* you know the truth?" Aiden asked her.

Her shoulders sagged, and she shook her head. "No, I don't. I don't know if Michelle and Rick were just saying that as some weird joke." She raised both palms. "I don't feel like I know anything."

"And that's the problem right now," Aiden agreed. "And we need to go talk to the detective about it."

She frowned and checked the wall clock. "At eight o'clock at night?"

"Do you really want to sit on the information?" Aiden asked her.

"Fine." At that, she got up and started to clear the table. She looked around and added, "You know that her father—stepfather—won't take this very kindly."

"I know," Aiden said, "but he could be in trouble of his own making for applying pressure to this case."

"Nobody will give a crap about that," she snapped, shaking her head. "He has been applying pressure for a very long time."

"Maybe that'll stop now." She gave him a hard look. He looked over at Mountain. "You'll stay here then?"

"No, I'll come with you," he stated, "because still, the best way to put all this to rest is to find out who killed the other six men."

"I don't understand why that isn't something that we already have answers for," she said, as she put away the food in the fridge. "I mean, aren't cameras everywhere around all those casinos?"

"There should be, and yet maybe our killer's just smart enough to stay out of the range of them."

"Then it's somebody local, who's already done a lot of scouting about town," she noted, "and that's just a shit deal too."

"In what way?"

"My first thought is, chances are, it's another dealer. They would be among the first to hear about the big winners and would be familiar with Vegas," she explained. "Yet I don't know for sure and can't prove that."

"Still, it's an interesting point that you bring up," Aiden noted. "Anybody hate you?"

"No, not that I know of. However, you know that possibly somebody else took out my ex at the same time as these other gamblers," she suggested. "That just made me look like a patsy and probably made them free and clear."

"Anybody you know doing very well financially all of a sudden?"

"Nobody is doing well financially."

"Anybody moving? Anybody buy a new car? Anybody give notice recently? Anybody do anything like that?"

She stopped and looked at him. "Can it be something so simple?"

"Absolutely," he confirmed. "Often this starts off as a necessity. They need something that they can't afford with their paycheck. Could be just enough money to pay the rent and their bills or could be worse, like cancer treatments or something. Could even be paying for their own drug habit or smoking habit or gambling habit—which they see as a *need* not as a *want*. Regardless, these people deem something as even more important in terms of money, and they scheme to get enough money to feed that desire. Then, all of a sudden, once they open that flood gate, they start seeing everything else they want in life."

"Right," she agreed, "which kind of sucks."

"Absolutely it sucks, but it doesn't change the fact that what they started off with doesn't mean that's what they expected to end up with. Maybe they had a grudge against the first guy who was killed."

At that, she winced. "You know what? That makes a little bit of sense too. The greedy money angle but also the revenge angle too."

# CHAPTER 13

A S TOBY AND Mountain silently watched, Aiden drove in the evening light up to the detective's house. They all approached the front door, and Aiden knocked.

The detective opened the front door, his hands at his hips, and glared at them. "This is pretty late for a visit. You could have called."

Aiden spoke up. "We have some more information that really doesn't work well over the phone."

With that, the detective sighed and motioned them inside. "Didn't they drop the charges?" he asked, focusing on Toby.

"Sure did," she replied, with a bright smile. But her smile fell away almost immediately.

He raised an eyebrow. "It's not making you as happy as I thought it would."

"Well ..." And then she stopped. Inside his office, he pointed at the visitor chairs, and the three of them arranged themselves around the detective's desk. "Now tell me. What's going on?" he asked.

She explained what had happened at lunch. His jaw dropped, and he stared at her seriously. She nodded. "Yeah, and we don't know what to do about that."

"Good God. And this is Moscow's sister, right?"

"Half sister." Toby nodded. "Yes, the one he's abused

psychologically for a very long time," she added. "I don't know if he also abused her sexually."

"Good God!" Still in shock, the detective frowned, as he sat here. "Is there anybody to ask?"

"No, not necessarily," Toby replied.

He stared at her for a moment. "Do you think Michelle understands what she did?"

"Do I think she understands what she did? Yes. Do I think she understands the repercussions of what she did? Absolutely not," she replied. "I suspect my *dearly beloved husband*," she added, with a sarcastic tone, "was hurting her, and she probably reacted reflexively."

He picked up his folder on Moscow's death. "You said that Moscow was stabbed to death?"

"No, that's what the cops told me."

He winced at that. "He died of a broken neck."

She stared at him in surprise.

"Any chance Michelle could have knocked him out of the window?"

"I don't know," she replied, her eyes closed, imagining the bedroom. "She is on the second floor, so I guess it's possible. I just don't know." Still working her imagination, she continued. "If that happened, what would she do?"

At that moment, Aiden immediately stepped up and stated, "She'd throw out the garbage."

The detective stared at him, his eyes widening. "Right. That is probably what she thinks she did."

"Yes," Toby murmured in agreement. "She would have indeed."

"Great," the detective replied. "I don't even know if the department can prove it."

"No, and I don't know is *we* can either," Toby noted,

"and I would be absolutely terrified of what would happen to her if it *was* proven."

"You don't think she should be punished for it?" Aiden asked Toby.

"No. Absolutely not," she stated. "Moscow made her life hell."

"But was he making her life hell at this time?" the detective asked, an eyebrow raised.

She shook her head. "I don't know, and I guess that makes a difference, doesn't it?"

"It's not always so cut-and-dried," the detective noted. "Certainly we have had cases where women have snapped after taking as much abuse as they can stand, and they've turned around and killed their abuser. But it's certainly not a common scenario, and I imagine each case creates its own problems."

"I would think so," Toby responded in a monotone, then shuddered. "It's already hard for me to live with what Michelle went through with Moscow, but now to think that there would be repercussions for it? I don't know how to handle that, to protect her from that."

"The question is whether she's a danger to anybody else," the detective noted.

"I know, right?" she agreed. "And I was thinking of that myself, but if nobody else in her life is abusing her, would it happen again?" Throwing up her hands, she added, "I don't know. I just don't know. ... I don't know if she even understands that Moscow's gone for good." She shook her head at that. "And I know that sounds pretty foolish too."

"No, it's not foolish," the detective confirmed, "but it would explain why his mode of death is so very different from the others. Speaking of which, the ballistics came back negative. Not related to anything in our database. Unfortunately, it could have helped lend weight to Moscow's character."

At that, she nodded in agreement.

Aiden spoke up. "On the way down here, I asked Toby if she knew anyone, another dealer in particular, who may have picked up some extra money, was flaunting money, or was looking like she or he was doing better than the others."

She replied with an abrupt no.

The detective nodded. "But is that a good line of questioning? It might not be somebody who's flaunting the money. They could be just stashing it until another time."

"I don't know anybody like that," she said. "Most of us are just working for a living. We make decent money to afford living in Vegas, but we certainly don't make an overwhelming amount of money."

"Well, if you did, none of you would still be there."

"Exactly," she agreed. They talked a little bit more, before getting ready to leave.

The detective added, "If you think of anything else, let me know."

"I will," she said. "The only dealer I know who bought something recently is Annabel, who bought a new car." She continued. "But then hers was a junker, and she needed a new one for a long time."

"Any idea how she would have paid for it?" Aiden asked.

"No, of course not," she replied. "How would I?"

"No idea," Aiden said, "but that is one of the red flags we were just talking about. If Annabel is somebody who doesn't spend a lot of money, that would be unusual."

"I don't know whether it's unusual or not," Toby countered. "I don't know her so well. I only know her from work, and I don't know what her life situation is. For all I know, she could have been saving for ten years."

Aiden nodded to that. "And that's a good point."

The detective stood and walked them to the front door. "I am in the process of dealing with all this other shit that you dumped on my lap. So I will talk to the right people about your sister-in-law."

Toby nodded slowly. "Thank you. I don't know what I can do about it."

"It's not necessarily something for you to do. It would be something that the DA—one of the assistants who can be trusted—will handle. And, of course, you don't have any proof yet that Michelle is involved." He looked at her intensely. "Or do you?"

She shook her head. "No, I don't. We tried to get her to talk further, but she was already off on a completely different topic."

"Yeah. Understood. Not to worry." The detective waved goodbye.

And, with that, they had to be satisfied. On the drive home, Toby whispered, "I feel like I've betrayed her."

"You can't feel that way. It doesn't help Michelle," Aiden said empathetically.

Toby's phone rang, with Michelle's name on the screen. "That's her now." She picked up the phone and answered. "Hey, Michelle. How are you doing?"

"Nightmares," she said, bawling.

"I'm so sorry, sweetie. More nightmares?"

"Yes," she muttered in fear. "He'll come back and hurt me, won't he?"

"No, he won't," she snapped, her voice sharp. "He won't come back anymore. That's over."

But it was too good to be true, as Michelle wouldn't listen, and she kept bawling.

At that moment, Aiden turned briefly toward Toby. "Do you want us to go over there?" She hesitated. "Not sure that would do anything," she whispered to Aiden. In empathy, she explained, "Michelle, you'll be okay. He's gone now."

"Yes," Michelle finally agreed, sniffling. "I don't like waking up in the night and seeing him there."

She froze. "That night?"

"That night," she agreed. "He was in my room. I didn't like that. He's not supposed to come in anymore."

"No, of course not," Toby agreed, putting her phone on Speaker so the others could hear.

Mountain put his phone on Record and leaned in closer.

"Michelle, what did Moscow do that night, when he visited your room afterhours at the group home?" she asked, ensuring all the relevant info was now being recorded.

"Like he always does, he hurt me!" Michelle wailed.

"Did he climb into your bed?" Toby asked.

At that moment, Michelle started to cry deep, wrenching sobs.

Toby gasped. "I'm so sorry, sweetheart," she said heartbreakingly. "He's been doing it for a long time, hasn't he?"

"Yes," Michelle whispered. "It needed to stop. Couldn't do it anymore."

"No, you shouldn't have to go through that. Moscow wasn't allowed to do that to you."

Michelle was hurt and unhappy, and she continued to cry deeply. Toby felt her own heart break, but, knowing she needed more answers, she asked, "Rick helped you, didn't he?"

"Yes," she mumbled. "He did. Rick heard my crying,

came to my room. And Rick is strong now. Really strong," she added. Then immediately her voice changed, and she said, "He's working out. Trying to protect me. Moscow bad man."

"He was a really bad man, sweetheart, a really bad man."

Then she started to cry again. "I didn't mean to hurt him."

"No, I'm sure you didn't," Toby agreed, her voice breaking. "Sometimes bad things happen to good people."

"Yes, I'm a good girl," Michelle said. "He should have stopped. I didn't want to hurt him."

"No, but you did hurt Moscow, didn't you?"

"Yes," she replied. "Rick grabbed Moscow, and I pushed him away. Rick came to stop him. Moscow was fighting Rick really hard, and I jumped up and grabbed Moscow's head. I told him to stop, to stop hurting me, to stop hurting Rick. Moscow finally stopped, but then he didn't move again."

Realizing a bit of progress, Toby asked, "And then you took him outside to the Dumpster, didn't you?"

"Rick did," she said. "I opened the doors, and we went outside with his body. Rick threw him over the fence, and then he jumped over and put Moscow in Dumpster." She was crying again. "It was wrong, wasn't it?"

"Yes, it was wrong," Toby noted. "However, I understand. I really do."

Michelle burst in tears, saying, "I don't want to live in jail. I'm a good girl."

"I know," Toby agreed. "You're a very good girl, and thank you for telling me."

At that moment, Michelle started to sob some more.

Toby didn't even know what to do. In the background she heard a voice.

"Put down the phone, honey. Come on. Let me get you something to help you sleep." Then Ann was on the other end. "Toby, is this you?"

"Yeah, it's me," she said.

"She's pretty overwrought, isn't she?" Ann asked. "Ever since her brother died."

"Tell her that I love her and that I'll talk to her tomorrow."

"Will do. I'll give her something to help her sleep tonight, and obviously we have to take it up with the doctor because this can't continue."

"No, of course not." Toby answered, "but maybe now she'll be a little calmer about it."

"Well, if she got a chance to talk to you, that might help her. She has been avoiding talking with any of us."

"No, we did talk a little bit," Toby admitted. "I hope it helped." And, with that, she rang off.

She stared down at her phone, tears in the corner of her eyes. She finally brushed them away, looked up at Aiden, and asked, "Now what?"

"It was self-defense," he said. "She won't get charged for something like that."

"Maybe," Toby said, feeling relief in her chest. "Michelle still has to deal with what happened. Trying to counsel somebody like her is just that much harder. In some ways, everything is so much simpler, and yet, in other ways, it's so much harder."

He nodded. "There are professionals who can help her."

She nodded. "I hope so because she deserves it. Her stepfather has the money to help but I don't think he will."

"You did mention that Moscow was paying her bills at the group home, right?"

She nodded. "Ann said the stepfather has never done anything to help Michelle. So I don't see that he would start now either."

"I don't know a lot on that topic," Aiden began, "but she's in a special group home, and I would think there should be some special financial assistance for her there."

"If I get Moscow's money, I'll take care of her. And I'd like to be her legal guardian. I don't even know if I can do that, what with recent murder charges." She frowned, deep in thought.

Aiden patted her hand. "Ask your attorney. Start there. Even one little step can help ward off some of the worries."

"Ann just said that Michelle only talks to me. Will she ever recover if she doesn't feel free to tell the professionals or even Ann at the home? Yet, if Michelle does tell them, that's likely to make things very different for her there. Difficult even."

"You can't solve all the world's problems tonight," Aiden noted. "Yet I think finding the right psychologist for her would change things for the better."

Just then, they pulled into her driveway. She looked up at the man there and groaned. "Dear God, like that's the last thing I need."

Aiden turned to look at the man on the steps. "Who is that?"

"My father-in-law," she snapped, with a certain bitterness that was hard to hide.

"Good," Aiden said, with a glance at Mountain in the back seat. "Let's get out and hear what he has to say."

"I really don't want to," she replied. "He scares me."

At that moment, Mountain looked at her and nodded. "You know something? This will be the last time he gets to scare you," Mountain stated. "We're here now. Don't forget that."

She nodded. "But he's also a big force in town."

Aiden asked, "Have you reconsidered moving somewhere else? It would be a really good time for you to start putting those plans in order."

"Do you think I can even leave?" she asked, now as she stepped from the vehicle. "You know? Because of the charges?"

"Everything was dropped."

"I don't think they'll let me leave town though," she said.

"Oh, they will. Particularly once the DA and everybody downwind of all this get their names in some damaging media coverage."

"And what about Michelle?" she whispered to Aiden. With a heavy sigh, Toby turned and walked up to her father-in-law. "Hello, Pia." He glared at her. "I didn't kill him, and you know that," she said.

"Bullshit!" he snapped. "I kept telling him how you were poison for him, but he wouldn't listen." He continued. "He kept saying that you were his. No matter what, you would be his."

She didn't say anything, but her heart sunk as she heard the threat in Pia's voice.

He looked past her at Aiden and Mountain behind her. And his gaze narrowed. "And who the hell are you?"

"I'm her cousin," Mountain replied, crossing his arms, looking at Pia in a relaxed manner.

"And I'm a friend of hers," Aiden said. "I understand that you've been packing quite a lot of threats and bullying tactics to get the police to charge her with something she didn't do."

"She killed my son!" he snapped. "Do you think I would sit by and let her get away with murder?"

"Except she didn't murder him and neither did the person who killed the six other gamblers as well."

"Well then, who did?" he asked balefully.

"Considering Moscow was blackmailing half the town, I don't think there'll be a shortage of suspects for the cops," she replied abruptly.

He spun on her. "He did not blackmail anybody."

"Well then, maybe you should go talk to the detective who is working on all the ledgers."

Aiden gave Pia the detective's name.

"Why would I want to do that?" Pia asked in disgust.

Aiden explained, "Because he's holding all Moscow's blackmail files and his little black book with all of it in there."

At that, Pia snapped back in anger. "What?"

"Yeah," Toby added, "so go ahead. Try and tell me that you didn't know anything about it because I saw emails in those files where you and Moscow talked all about it. So, if I were you, I would be thinking more about what you want to save of your reputation and maybe thinking to relocate somewhere else," she suggested, "before the charges start flying that you were in cahoots with your son's blackmailing scheme."

He stared at her and replied with a note of fury in his voice, "What the hell are you talking about?"

But she wouldn't be stopped. "I know exactly what I'm talking about." She glared at him. "You're despicable. All you ever do is live on threats and hunt people down and make their lives miserable." She stared at him with such fury that he backed up a step. "As far as I'm concerned, the cops can take you down and throw away the key for all the times that you've hurt other people in this town. Your son was a rapist and a lowlife slug who preyed on vulnerable people. So don't go talking to me about your *best son ever* bullshit!" she snapped. "I'm totally okay if his reputation comes out, and people finally know exactly what he was like and that you're okay with that, that you were grooming him to do more and more of the same."

He took another step back. "I don't know what you're talking about," he said, but his face was pale, as if he only now started to realize that he could be in jeopardy himself.

"Oh, yeah, you do," she called his bluff. "Now get the hell off my property, before I file trespassing charges against you. Then go ahead and try to again manipulate the local law enforcement against me," she snapped. "I am no longer without friends and support, and your brand of bullying persuasion is over at the DA's office, and now the DOJ will deal with you," she stated in a harsh voice. "Honestly I hope they throw the book at you for everything."

He took several more steps back, shaking his head. "You don't know what you're talking about."

"Yeah, I do. Moscow left detailed notes," she shared. "We haven't even gotten through everything yet."

He stared at her and took a deep breath. "Moscow wouldn't have done that."

"Yes, he would have. Believe me. As long as he was alive and well, it was fine. He could control things. However, the minute he died, that all changed. And I got curious about all the stuff he left behind with me." She continued. "After you had me charged for a crime I didn't commit, you can bet I found somebody trustworthy in the police system that you can't bribe or threaten, just so that I get a fair shake. The murder charges against me have been dropped, by the way," she added. "Stay tuned for charges against you now." She continued glaring at him.

"I just wanted Moscow to be happy," he said, staring at her.

"No, you didn't. You wanted him to control me, and you wanted to control Moscow. However, he was a wild card, who abused even his poor sister, Michelle."

He waved a hand. "That's BS. She's been spouting all that crap forever. There's no proof of it."

"Yes, there is," she argued. "And now Moscow won't be abusing anybody anymore, and, for that, I'm glad. The fact that you can live with the knowledge that your son abused his half sister all these years?" She shook her head. "Of course, for a manipulating bully like you, that's nothing, right? I mean, in your patriarchal mind-set, that's how women are supposed to be treated, *right*?" With a disgusted look, she added, "You're nothing, but guess what? Your day of reckoning is here," she vowed.

He took several more steps away. "You're lying," he said, obviously shaken.

"No, I'm not lying," she countered, "but you can bet, by the time I sell everything of Moscow's and clean out his apartment and do everything else that needs to be done, I'll find more and more pieces that need to come out into the light, into the public's purview."

He shook his head. "No, you can't do that."

"Why not?" She shrugged, with a sneer. "It's not like you can stop me."

"I wanted to keep his apartment," he said painfully. "There's very little I have of my son to keep."

"You can buy it from me then," she stated sarcastically. He glared at her, and she shook her head. "No, he insisted I marry him, so I'll make sure I end up with something out of this deal, so I can move and start somewhere else."

"And where will you move to?" he asked, dazed.

"What do you care?" she snapped. "I just want to make sure that I'm nowhere close to you."

He shook his head. "It's all just a lie, isn't it?" He turned, looking at the men. "What she just said, it's a lie. Right?"

AT THAT, AIDEN shook his head. "No, it isn't. Unfortunately it's all very true. And we have evidence to back up everything Toby just told you. Moscow sexually abused Michelle in the group home, and he has made Toby's life here an absolute nightmare."

Pia's face turned gray, and he shuddered. "I didn't know," he murmured.

"You defended every depraved thing that Moscow ever did," she snapped. "And I wouldn't be at all surprised if you weren't charged over all this blackmail too."

Immediately Pia shook his head. "My lawyers will work on that in no time," he murmured, regaining some strength in his voice.

"An awful lot of evidence was turned over to the detective, then to the DOJ," she noted, with a headshake. "So I wouldn't count on it."

He nodded slowly, and, in a much more haggard frame of mind, Pia slowly made his way back to his vehicle. Once there, he turned to Toby and said, "I'll have my lawyers contact you."

She waited—not sure what for.

When he saw the confusion on her face, he added, "The apartment. I do want it."

She nodded. "You're welcome to it, for the right price. Do you want his personal stuff left as is inside?"

He looked at her and then nodded. "Yes, please."

"Fine. Make the arrangements," Toby replied.

And, with that, Pia got in his vehicle and drove away.

She looked over at the guys and asked, "Was that wrong?"

"No, not at all," Aiden noted. "Legally you seem entitled to it."

"It just feels wrong," she explained, still in a confused state.

Mountain shook his head. "You need a fresh start. He's got tons of money. He wants to keep the apartment, when it is legally yours. Let the lawyers handle it, take the best offer possible, and then you can set up someplace new."

"And where will you go?" Aiden asked, eyeing her carefully.

She smiled. "I have no idea."

"Good," Aiden said. "In that case, you might as well come back to my place for a while, until you figure it out." She stared at him, her mouth agape. He shrugged. "Hey, don't tell me that we haven't been dancing around the same tune," he noted. "You obviously just need some time, and I'm giving you time."

"Oh, yeah? How much time are you giving me?" she asked in a mocking tone. "Doesn't sound like very much time at all."

"I'll give you as much time as you need," he stated, with

a big smile.

"Besides, I don't even know where you live," she replied, frowning at him.

"California."

"Oh, … I was considering California."

He now gave her a beaming smile. "So, I'm not kidding. You can come stay with me for a while."

"And I might take you up on that," she murmured. "But we're not past all this mess, are we?"

"Nope, not yet," he agreed. "There is one thing I do want to know."

"What's that?" she asked.

"Where does this girlfriend of yours live?"

"Which one?"

"Annabel, the one who took the picture of your bruised body."

"She's not far from here. She lives close to the casino. She's got a single bedroom apartment with her boyfriend."

"What's her boyfriend like?" he asked.

"He's a bouncer at the casino," she noted absentmindedly.

"So he's big?"

"Yeah, big and strong, one of those heavily muscled guys," she said. "He's kind of nosy though. He's always got his nose sticking into other people's business."

"As in, he might have been able to keep track of who made big wins in the casino?"

"Sure," she agreed. "I'm certain he did. Lots of people do there." He nodded and searched her face. And then she frowned at him, as if suddenly understanding what he was getting at. "You can't be serious?"

"Why not?" he asked.

"Sure, she bought a car, but that's it."

"What kind of car?"

"I don't know, just a car."

"A fancy car, a sports car?" he asked anxiously.

"I don't know. I didn't ask. I couldn't care less. We were having a conversation. I was happy she managed to buy a vehicle—something that most of us still struggle with. And, if she got one, then good for her."

"And you know what her vehicle looks like?"

She shook her head. "Never saw it. Not the old one and not this new one."

Still not satisfied, he asked, "Do you know what her boyfriend's name is?"

She gave Aiden the bouncer's full name and Annabel's last name. He quickly sent both to Corbin and asked for identification on the vehicle newly purchased. When that intel came back almost immediately, Aiden stared down at it and said, "We may want to go inside."

"Why is that?" she asked, but she was already unlocking her front door and going in. "God, it has been a strange day. I'm still in shock over Michelle."

"And we need to take that over to the detective too," Aiden noted.

"What?" She looked at him.

"Yeah, the recording Mountain made of your telephone conversation with Michelle," Aiden explained. "It saves you the time to remember all the details. It's also much more powerful, hearing Michelle's own voice share the facts."

Toby winced at what they were talking about. "No, you're right. It's just heartbreaking."

"It is, indeed, but that's also why it's very important that we have a record of Michelle's statement."

As Toby stepped into the living room and dropped her purse on the side table, she asked, "Now what are you talking about with the vehicle?"

"So, the bouncer didn't buy a sports car, but he got a very high-end Escalade," Aiden shared with both of them. "So that was a $120,000 vehicle."

"Or maybe they took a loan out?" she asked, her jaw still dropping.

"I doubt it. According to Corbin's research, it was bought at a dealership, but I'm waiting to hear how it was paid for." His phone beeped again. "And look at that. It was paid for in cash."

She shook her head. "That's not exactly the vehicle that I would have thought she'd buy."

"No, and, unless they can justify where that cash money came from, believe me. There'll be an awful lot of raised eyebrows."

"Not really though," she argued. "I never saw it once."

"Are they staying in town?"

"No, I don't think so," she said. "They were planning on leaving soon. She always wanted to go west."

"Of course," Aiden quipped. "And, with a vehicle like that, they would have a nice trip."

She sagged into the nearest chair. "Do you think she's killing those guys?"

"How badly do they want or need cash?"

"Badly, from what I hear. Annabel has definitely got a money problem and has a real attitude about it. She hates people with money," she muttered. "It's one of the reasons that we got along, okay? I didn't have any either."

"How much does she hate rich people?"

She winced in realization. "Oh my God. That would be

terrible."

Just then Aiden's phone rang. He checked the screen and said, "It's the detective. Now maybe we can get some real answers."

# CHAPTER 14

"Hey," Aiden answered the phone. "I was about to contact you. I have a recording of a discussion with Michelle, where she admits to sexual abuse from Moscow and to killing him." He nodded and glanced at Mountain, who, as they shared a knowing look, sent the recording from Mountain's phone over to Aiden's cell.

"Send that to me," the detective noted. "And we've just checked into Annabel. She does have an alibi for the might of the murders. Her boyfriend."

"Interesting," Aiden said in a low voice, looking at Toby. "Because we found out from the DMV that the vehicle she just bought was an Escalade." The detective whistled at the other end. Aiden continued. "Annabel's boyfriend is a bouncer who also works at the same casino." He handed over their names and added, "I'll email you this recording of Michelle. It was self-defense though."

"I'm glad to hear that. We'll do a review, and I'll get back to you on it. And what are you doing about Annabel?" the detective asked.

"We'll question her. I understand the local cops already have picked her up for an interview with them. I'll go down and talk to her."

"Anything else happening on the rest of this?" he asked.

"Lots," he replied cheerfully. "Toby's father-in-law was

here, waiting for us. So he knows we know he was in on the blackmailing scheme. However, he didn't seem to know about his son sexually attacking Michelle."

"But you know a lot of it will entail internal investigations," the detective reminded Aiden.

"And a lot of it shouldn't be internal, given the dirty cops and the dirty DA."

"No, but I'm sure it'll come out soon enough," the detective shared. "However, we need to keep it under wraps for the moment."

"But *for the moment* you can," Aiden agreed. "Yet no way we're letting this get pushed under the rug for long, not when Toby was charged so quickly with no evidence for something that she had nothing to do with."

"Yeah, I figured you guys wouldn't like that much."

"No, we sure don't," Aiden snapped. "There will be justice."

"You bet," the detective added. With that, he hung up.

Aiden looked over at the others. "That was Henry. Annabel does have an alibi for those nights that the six other gamblers were murdered. Get this though. The alibi is her bouncer boyfriend. Supposedly they were at home each of those nights."

"Of course," Toby said. "That makes sense to me." She frowned as she studied Aiden's expression. "Yet I can't believe you're thinking that she might have done these killings just for the money."

"I'm not necessarily thinking she did," Aiden corrected her. "I'm just saying that, using the exact same logic the cops used on you, it applies to her too."

"Oh no," she muttered. "Her motive would be money, with the evidence being her brand-new Escalade, and her accomplice is her boyfriend. So, you're right there." She slowly turned her head. "This is a fine mess, isn't it?"

"It is." He quickly sent the tape recording he had from his phone to Henry's. "And I just sent him the conversation with Michelle and told him it was clear-cut case of self-defense."

"If anything is *clear-cut* with her," she muttered. "I just hope that there aren't repercussions that we'll struggle with here."

"We'll always struggle with a certain amount of it," her cousin noted.

She nodded. "I just don't want any more of that shit to come down."

"Well, first off," Aiden suggested, "let's make plans for a late-night snack or something that completely takes some of this off your mind."

She shook her head. "Not possible." She gave him a wry look. "Just too much going on."

"Fine, but let us still plan something at home for tonight, where we can all relax, because you know that there is a chance we'll lose Mountain here very quickly."

"A big chance at that," Mountain admitted.

"Have you heard more?" Toby asked him.

He nodded. "Just nothing confirmed yet," he said, but his tone was dark.

"Is your brother mixed up in something ugly?"

"Well, he went there to investigate something that was ugly. Yes. Two of his friends are there, and they're the ones who raised the alarm, so we managed to get him inside the training center, where this is all happening, but it could be that it has turned on him."

"That's not good," Toby said.

"I know, but the whole investigation could be a long process. It's a joint task force up north in the Arctic. They resurrected an old encampment and multiple compound buildings for this big training facility," Mountain explained. "We've got representatives from Norway, Germany, Poland, and other nations up there."

She stared at her cousin, her eyes huge. "And who's in the wrong there?"

"Not sure anybody is," he stated. "That's the problem."

"And you haven't heard back from your brother?"

"No, not at the moment," he replied. "So far, nobody on the ground up there has heard from him."

"Oh, shit," she said, staring at him. "I don't like the sound of that at all."

"He went out on a reconnaissance mission, as part of a training program. Everybody else came back, but he didn't. The search party is out there now."

She shook her head. "Dear God, in those temperatures? No way to survive for long in those severe conditions."

"You'd be surprised," Mountain argued, with a quiet tone. "Surviving is one thing, but doing it well is a different story. Other people are around up there. A small town is nearby, so my brother could be anywhere."

"Of course he could," she agreed, "and, if he's as good as you say he is, then there's a good chance that he's doing just fine."

He smiled at that. "He is a different man. I can promise you that."

"Because you say that then, I'll believe you. I just know everything from his past."

"And sometimes you have to let a man let that go," Mountain suggested.

"If you say so," she muttered.

But, at that moment, Aiden hopped to his feet, reached out a hand to Toby, and said, "Come on. Let's go find a snack or dessert." She let him pull her to her feet, as he wrapped an arm around her shoulders. "You'll love California."

She shook her head. "I'm coming as a friend," she warned.

He chuckled. "The way things are between us, the friendship will turn into something much deeper, much quicker."

"Says you," she protested. "I didn't say I was interested in a relationship."

"You don't have to," he noted. "Your body already says so."

"That's bullshit," she murmured.

"No, not at all." He reached over and kissed her gently on the temple. "Remember. No pressure. You had enough of that shit from Moscow."

"You're not kidding," she agreed. "I haven't had a relationship in a long time because of him too, so I won't be too eager to jump into another."

"Unless you're really eager to jump into it because, you know, maybe you'll really enjoy it this time."

"I'll enjoy the fact that I'm free to have a relationship again."

"Did he really hound everybody who you know?"

"In so many ways," she said, nodding her head. "He just made life miserable. I was out on a date one night, and he beat up the guy at the restaurant."

"And nobody pressed charges?" he asked in shock.

"No, once my date had been thoroughly threatened, he

took off, and I've never seen him again," she explained. "I'm pretty sure he was in town only for a few days and hasn't come back to the city since."

"You can understand his point though, I'm sure?" he noted. "However, I don't scare so easily."

She smiled up at him. "You really are a nice man, you know that?"

"I am," he stated, "and you'll learn just how nice I am as time goes on."

She nodded. "The only reason I'm even taking the chance with you is because Mountain vouched for you."

"And I also know that, if I do anything to cross those lines with you, Mountain'll kick my butt into tomorrow," Aiden confessed, with a laugh. "I know it. You know it, and that keeps everything aboveboard."

"Sure," she said, "but what happens if I fall for you and if I treat you badly?"

"Then Mountain will kick *your* butt all the way into tomorrow," he teased, not missing a beat. "But I'm looking forward to you trying."

She burst out laughing.

He looked down at her and grinned. Reaching over, he kissed her gently and repeated, "Honestly, no pressure."

"That's a good thing," she said, "because I wasn't really thinking about such a thing."

"Yes, you were," he argued, with a smile. "But that's okay, I'll let you believe it."

She shook her head. "Are you always this determined?"

"Yep," he said, then turned to his buddy. "Am I right, Mountain?"

"He's not kidding," Mountain muttered from behind them.

Aiden looked over at his friend and realized that Mountain was quite distracted by his phone. He turned to Toby. "Come on," he said. "Mountain needs a healthy distraction. Let's get together a late-night snack." And, with that, he now dragged Mountain into the kitchen, and they grabbed grapes and cheese from the fridge and some nuts and dark chocolate from her pantry.

"It seems like we're always eating," she noted cautiously.

"I can eat," Aiden said, with a shrug.

"Being able to eat doesn't mean it's the same thing as being hungry," she argued in a scolding voice.

"Mountain, can you eat?" he asked.

"Absolutely," Mountain declared. "About time you mentioned it."

"Hey, we already had dinner. Remember how I cooked for you two?" she noted.

"I remember. It was steak and corn and really tasty," Mountain said, looking at her. "What does that have to do with anything? I'm still hungry."

She threw up her hands. "Maybe that's why your parents didn't want anything to do with you," she said in a joking voice. "You just ate them out of house and home."

"Yeah, what about your parents?"

At that, she stopped and winced. "God. You know that we need to leave for California before they find out that somebody else has the blackmail info—or worse that the cops have the blackmail stuff now and where it came from— because my parents won't be nice to me."

"Well, they won't get to you in California in that case," Aiden stated immediately.

She smiled. "Now I like the sound of that. You have no idea how reassuring it is to know that somebody's in my corner."

"I understand," Aiden said. "I've been alone in my lifetime too. That's why people like Mountain are important in my world."

"That's what real friends are for. I guess I missed that stage," she noted thoughtfully. "And that was another side effect of Moscow. He wouldn't let anybody be my friend. I was his, and he wouldn't share, and that was it."

"But he's gone, so it doesn't matter anymore."

"I know. I know," she said, "and every time I remember that, it's just a huge sigh of relief. It's just going to take a while before all his abuse fades away, and I can really relax. In a way, I'm like Michelle. Not quite believing the boogeyman is gone."

"And will you be okay if we move away, with Michelle still here?"

She frowned at that and then slowly nodded. "It would be hard, but she can still talk to me on the phone. Plus we can come back and see her. It would be harder on her if she didn't have Rick."

"Or maybe you can also find a place in California so that she'd be closer too."

She shook her head. "She's got really good friends in the group home here, and that's important to her."

"And that's what happens in life," Aiden stated. "Maybe you'll find that now that she's had a chance to tell her story and that this is out of her life, maybe she'll settle in and gain more friends."

"I think so. She's really lovable," Toby said warmly. "I just don't know how she'll handle me moving."

"Well, let's not cross that bridge right now," Aiden noted. "And, if necessary, you know that we'll reassess it down the road."

She looked up at him.

He smiled. "I'm really easy to get along with."

"You're almost too easy to get along with," she replied shrewdly. "It's almost like you have an agenda."

"The only agenda I have is to keep you happy, safe, and around me," he shared. "Everything else is secondary."

She looked over at Mountain and asked, "Is he really like this?"

Mountain nodded. "Absolutely. All the time, every day, it's that bloody happy puppy look. Pretty sickening, isn't it?"

At that instant, a grape hit Mountain in the head. He spun so fast, but Aiden was already out of sight.

"See? That's what I mean," Mountain complained. "The guy is just a walking joke."

"And yet obviously you two love each other like brothers."

"We do," Mountain agreed, with a nod. "Because, when you find somebody like this, you hang on to them. I know that, if I run into trouble up north and if I need to have Aiden bail me out, he'd come."

"In a heartbeat," Aiden added immediately, rejoining them, "because that's what friends do." He looked over at her and added, "It's okay. You'll learn too. You might not have a whole lot of confidence in that whole process, but you'll learn to trust it."

"Maybe," she said. "Right now, I'll have to take your word for it."

Just then a knock came at her front door. The door opened, and a woman stepped in, calling out, "Hey, anybody here? Toby, you here?" She stopped in the kitchen, staring at the men.

"This is Annabel," Toby said to the guys. "She's the one who sent the picture of the bruises on my back."

Immediately Aiden stepped forward and said, "Hey, this is a surprise."

Toby stared at her friend. "Are you okay?" Obviously Annabel had been crying.

Annabel shook her head. "No, I'm not really okay." She glared at Toby. "All because of you, yet I even went to bat for you."

"What are you talking about?" Toby asked in confusion.

"You told the cops that I killed those men," Annabel said in a hurt tone.

"I did no such thing," she protested immediately.

But Annabel wasn't listening. "They told me that."

"Of course they did," she snapped in disgust. "Remember? The cops lie."

"No, they told me that you didn't kill them, and, therefore, you pointed the finger at me," she complained. "I don't understand how you could do that. We're friends."

"Sure we are," Toby agreed, frowning, not sure where it was all going. "But I didn't tell them that. They asked me if anybody had bought a new vehicle, and I said you did, but I didn't know anything about it. I couldn't even tell them what vehicle it was."

Annabel looked at her suspiciously. And then she turned to the two men behind her. "Who are these guys?"

"This is my cousin, Mountain," Toby said, "and this is Aiden, a friend of mine. I mean it, Annabel," Toby continued. "I didn't do anything more than that. And what am I supposed to say when they asked who else bought new vehicles recently?"

Annabel shook her head. "I told him that we shouldn't

buy a vehicle right now, but he didn't listen."

"I didn't know buying a vehicle was a problem at any time," Toby admitted.

"Well, it is because he shouldn't have done it," she snapped, "but he never listens."

"I'm sorry," Toby said. "I didn't mean to cause you any trouble."

She stared at her and shrugged, yet still glared at Toby. "You *did* bring us a lot of trouble. It makes me so sorry that I gave you that photo."

"Why?"

"Because it got you off the hook."

"No, it didn't," she countered. "But I had an alibi for the latest murder, so they could hardly charge me for that. Plus they had absolutely no forensic evidence on me," she stated in disgust. "My father-in-law was pushing for me to be charged."

Annabel stared at Toby. "You married that louse?"

"Yeah, and then he was killed. I mean, if the same person killed Moscow who killed the other six now, I almost want to thank him, but I don't think it was the same person."

"The cops were talking about all these murders and questioning me," she stated, frowning.

"I know because I went through it earlier, and it's terrifying," Toby explained, "but the cops lied to you. That was not on me."

"Crap! But you haven't been honest with me," she said, pointing to the guys. "I didn't know about your boyfriend here, but then I didn't know about your husband either." She shook her head. "Just what a shitstorm. After just a simple thing like buying a new car."

"Where were you planning on moving to?" Toby asked, trying to distract her.

"It doesn't matter now," Annabel snapped. "We have to get clear of this mess first."

"Yeah, you do. Running right now won't be a good thing in the eyes of the cops."

"Maybe not, but you know I won't stick around for them to stick these five murders on us."

At the word *five*, Toby stared at Annabel. "Five?"

"Yeah, five," she repeated.

"I thought they were talking about six total murders now, not counting Moscow's."

The woman flushed. "I don't know what the hell they were talking about. Anyway I'm out of here."

But Toby opened her arms and headed toward her, and Annabel stepped back. "Don't even begin to pull that shit with me," she said. "You're not stopping me."

"I'm wasn't thinking that," Toby argued. "I was going to hug you goodbye."

Annabel reached into her purse and pulled out a small handgun. "Yeah, sure you were," she said in disgust.

Toby came to jittery stop. "What are you doing?"

"Well, if you're trying to accuse me of something," she stated, "I'm not having it. And don't bother trying to follow me. I hope to never see you again," Annabel spat, and, with that, she bolted outside.

Aiden followed immediately and checked out her vehicle. "Yes, it's an Escalade." He pulled out his phone and immediately called Henry. "So your murderer just took off in the Escalade. You may want to get out an APB, as they're planning on leaving town as soon as possible." With that, he hung up and looked over at Toby. "See? That was pretty simple."

"I don't think so," she disagreed and pointed. At that instant, the Escalade pulled up in front of her house again. "There she is again."

But, instead of the woman, the big bouncer popped out, and he raced up the front steps. He smiled and started firing blindly at them. She bolted toward the couch, as Aiden tackled her; she felt a pull on her shoulder and started swearing. More shots were fired into windows and doors, flying all around.

"That'll teach you fuckers to not get involved where you shouldn't be," he yelled, and, with that, he jumped in the Escalade and raced off down the street.

AIDEN PULLED OUT his phone and called for an ambulance. At the same time, he put pressure on Toby's wound. He looked over at Mountain, who raced toward them. "She took one shot," Aiden noted, "at least that's all I can see."

Mountain quickly checked over his cousin. "Looks like it," he said, checking the wound closer. "It's high in the shoulder, but she's bleeding pretty heavily."

By the time the ambulance reached them, they had the bleeding somewhat slowed, but she was unconscious. They quickly got Toby loaded up and down to the hospital.

On the way there, Aiden phoned Henry and then Corbin. "Things have blown up like you wouldn't believe." He quickly explained.

Henry met Aiden at the hospital. "We got both of them," he stated. "Don't worry. We got the escalade too. At the moment, Annabel's pissed that her boyfriend came in and shot at all of you, but she's the one who drove him back to Toby's house to do the dirty deed. So both of them are in jail, and one is singing like a canary."

"Which one is that?"

Henry shook his head. "Doesn't matter because, by the time I'm done with them, they'll both be singing."

"Fun times," Aiden noted. "Meanwhile, Toby's in surgery, getting that bullet removed from her shoulder."

"That's good," Henry noted.

"Maybe," Aiden agreed, "but, at the same time, the fact that Toby even got shot is bullshit. The bouncer fired dozens of shots into her house, so, in one way, at least that was the worst of it."

"I know," Henry noted. "All I can tell you is it's over now."

"Not fully," Aiden argued, "but you know we're getting there."

"I did talk to the *new* DA," he shared. "No charges will be filed against Michelle, but they will talk with her and will have a therapist work with her. Michelle has to know what she did was wrong and that she can't be allowed to ever do anything like that again."

"That will make Toby feel much better."

"Even with Michelle here, I'm surprised Toby's planning on staying here," the detective said.

"She's not. She'll sell her husband's apartment to her father-in-law, and then she's coming out west with me," Aiden shared. "The best thing for her is to get her out of here."

"I agree," Henry stated. "It's been a pretty rough ride for her."

"You're not kidding," Aiden agreed. "I just need to get

her out of surgery and well enough to travel."

At that, the detective took his leave from the hospital, and Aiden sat back down again.

Mountain had gone out to make a phone call, and he returned and sat down beside Aiden.

"When are you leaving?" Aiden asked.

"I don't know," Mountain replied. "I just put a call into the Mavericks."

"Why the Mavericks?"

"Like I said, I need somebody who can operate within yet on the edge of the law. And I need supplies and support. I also need a team. And Corbin is working on it," Mountain added. "When we get there, we'll need you too."

"Do you want me to go north?" Aiden asked.

"No, I won't need you on the ground in that op," Mountain noted. "I want you to stay here and to look after my cousin, to get her moved out west, to help her sell all this Moscow shit, to bank whatever money she can bank, and to start over out there in California. I have no idea what her parents will do, but I expect they will probably just ignore her. So she definitely needs a fresh start."

"She'll get it," Aiden stated, without hesitation.

"Oh, one more thing," Mountain added. "Corbin had the local retired military guy check out the safety deposit box and also the rented storage unit. Both filled with cash. Our local guy's changing the lock on the storage unit, and he has the paperwork to change the signee on the bank box, all while Corbin consults a local attorney. Then, if all goes well, that money will be transferred into Toby's account or go to some investment firm or whatever she decides."

"Sounds good," Aiden replied. He looked over at his buddy and added, "It's you who I'm worried about now."

Mountain directed a glare at him. "And with good reason. It's a nightmare out there."

"Is it really bad?"

"I can't tell you all the details, but I can tell you that it looks like we've got somebody taking out multiple people and some sort of international espionage going on." Mountain grimaced as he shook his head. "I know of four deaths, and I'm afraid my brother will be the fifth. I have to go out and find him."

"Understood," Aiden replied. "It sounds like a rough go to have you here when you so want to be there for your brother."

"It'll be an ugly international op, and it won't happen fast enough," Mountain stated. "Everybody on my team will have to infiltrate the global training system to figure out what's going on. We don't know who the hell's killing people or why those individuals were targeted. We don't know if this is an attempt to make it look like somebody else is murdering these trainees. So far, everything just looks like an accident. But, in three months, there have been four *accidents*. And now my brother remains missing."

"Right," Aiden agreed. "So no accident."

"Exactly," Mountain stated.

The doctor stepped out of the surgery room, searching for someone, and asked, "Are you Aiden?"

"I am," he confirmed and stood.

"Good. She'll be fine. She's coming out now to be transferred to her private room. You'll see her in a couple hours." He added, "I suspect she'll be okay to go home in a couple days."

"Perfect," Aiden replied. "You have any problems with her going home to California in another week or so?"

"No, but I'd like to see Toby once more—or you can take her to her California doctor for the stitches to be removed," he instructed. "However, I'm currently more worried about the next twenty-four hours." With that, the doctor took off.

Aiden looked around but found no sign of Mountain. Almost immediately Toby was brought down the hallway, and Aiden followed, without any of the nurses noticing or stopping him. While they went inside one of the patient rooms, he stayed out of the way to ensure that nobody would have a problem with his presence.

As soon as they left Toby alone in her new hospital room, he sat down beside her bed. The room was quiet finally, and he whispered, "Hey, you make sure you get better, so we can have a life together."

Instead of opening her eyes, Toby let a small smile play at the corner of her lips. "You know that's not a bad thing to wake up to," she replied, "because I feel pretty shitty right now."

"You should be pretty high on the drugs," Aiden noted, laughing.

"No, I hear you," she murmured. "That's … Wow, I wasn't expecting to be shot."

"They did catch him."

"Both of them?" she asked, opening her eyes, rolling her head ever-so-slightly to the side.

"Yeah, both of them. And, from the text I just got from Henry, they've both confessed, and the cops have found their stash of the rest of the cash they took off those six guys."

She smiled. "So they both confessed to murdering everybody?"

"Everybody but your ex."

"Right." Toby sighed. "Because of course that was

Michelle."

Aiden nodded. "However, it also looks like the new DA won't bring any charges against your sister-in-law. It was self-defense. They'll arrange therapy and make sure that she understands the gravity of what happened, and she'll be in the clear."

"Good," she whispered, with relief. "And me?"

"The doc just wants to make sure you get through the night, okay? No extra bleeding or infection or whatever. And then, if everything looks good," he added, "you might be released tomorrow or the day after."

"Even better," she murmured, as she closed her eyes.

"I asked the doc if he had a problem with you traveling to California right away."

Her eyes popped open. "Right away?"

"Yeah, right away sounds good to me," he stated. "This town is definitely not good for you."

"I have to deal with my father-in-law first."

"Nope, you don't. All he has to do is get his lawyers to send your attorney the paperwork, and it can be done and dealt with from a distance, just between the lawyers."

"I'll still be in rough shape for a while."

"Remember. No pressure."

"I remember that," she whispered, closing her eyes again. "Thank you for that."

"As long as you haven't changed your mind."

Her eyes slowly opened, and she gave him one of the sweetest smiles he'd ever seen. "Nope, I haven't changed my mind ... unless you have."

"Nope, I sure haven't," he declared. "If I could safely swoop you up and take you out of here right now, I would."

"Maybe tomorrow," she murmured, with a ghost of a smirk on her lips. "Right now I'll just sleep."

# CHAPTER 15

TOBY WOKE UP and smiled at the beautiful sunshine entering their bedroom. Slipping on her bathing suit, she walked out to the pool in Aiden's backyard.

He sat there with a cup of coffee. "Hey, sunshine."

"Hey," she said. "I can't believe it's been two weeks already."

"Yeah, and yesterday the local doctor cleared you, so you know everything's healing nicely."

"Yeah, it's still pretty sore," she complained good-naturedly.

"It won't be forever, and we'll have to work on making sure you stretch that shoulder and can move it without pain eventually and all that good stuff," he explained. He got up and gave her a gentle hug.

"You've been very patient."

He shook his head. "No, not at all. I'm not here for the short-term. I'm here for the long-term."

"And those are," she murmured, "some of the nicest words I've ever heard."

He kissed her softly and said, "Swim first, then I'll fix breakfast."

"I—" Her gaze checked out his basically nude body, wearing just his swim trunks. "I was wondering about, you know, maybe a *nap*."

His eyes widened. "Are you that tired?" he asked.

"No, not at all," she replied. "I am feeling much better." And, with that, she unhooked the top of her bathing suit and dropped it to the ground. She pulled the two tie strings on the sides of her bikini, then turned and walked away.

"Holy shit," Aiden said. "Are you trying to give me a heart attack?" As he came up behind her, he scooped her into his arms and carried her right through to their bedroom.

She laughed and looped her arm around his shoulders. "Well, you know what? For the last couple days I've been thinking we were ready for this, but you've been *oh so honorable*," she teased, with an eye roll.

"Hey, I promised I wouldn't push."

"Yeah, you did, so I figured I would have to do something a little more obvious."

"Well, you did." He carefully laid her on the bed and shucked off his trunks. He came down gently on the bed beside her. "Are you sure you are ready now?"

"If you turn me down, it'd be really hard for me to get over the rejection," she murmured, with a glint in her eyes.

He looked at her in shock, "I could never do that to you."

"I don't know," she quipped. "Sounds like you were really close to asking me if I was serious or whether I would change my mind."

He smiled. "I'd never insult you like that."

"That's good," she stated, her gaze warming. "So what are you wasting all this time for? Haven't we wasted enough?"

"I don't know that we've wasted any of it," he argued. "We've played chess, poker, Monopoly, and backgammon. We've read books, watched movies, and laughed. We even cried and talked until we're blue in the face," he replied. "That sounds like time well spent to me. Honestly I think those were some of the nicest times I've ever spent with a woman," he confessed.

"You mean because we hadn't been making love?"

"Well, not exactly. I was really looking forward to that part," he teased, with a wicked grin. "But remember. No pressure."

She pulled him to her so that they were skin to skin, chest to chest, and whispered. "Well, there's pressure now," she noted, "but only a pressure which you can satisfy."

He lowered his head and whispered, "Your wish is my command." And kissed her.

By the time he raised his head again, she could barely focus on the beloved face in front of her. "Wow. If I knew *that* was waiting for me all this time, I would have gotten here faster."

"No, it was better this way," he said. He gently dropped kisses across her cheek and down the nape of her neck, while she twisted beneath him. Then he explored the long slim body in front of him. "And remember," he added, "we have all the time in the world."

"No, we don't. We have a whole lot of life out there that I want to experience. I feel like I've waited on so much in so many ways that I don't want to wait anymore—for any of these experiences with you."

When he took her nipple deep into his mouth, she arched beneath him, shuddering. "Dear God."

He did it again and again, and each time she felt her body responding. She spread her legs and wrapped them around his hips, while trying to bring him up higher so that she could kiss him. When he wouldn't comply, she looped her fingers through his hair and tugged gently. When he moved to her other breast, she gave up all pretenses and just moaned beneath his ministrations.

As he made his way down to her belly, she cried out and sat up, pulling him toward her so that she could kiss him soundly. He immediately shifted his position, so he was sitting on the bed and pulled her onto his lap. With his erection firm and proud between them, he said, "We can do it this way, if you want."

She looked at him, then downward, and smiled. Immediately her hands slowly wrapped around his shaft in front of her.

He shuddered and mumbled, "Or not … because *you* might have time for this, but I'm not sure I'll make it." She smiled as she gently stroked a finger over the moisture at the top. He moaned and flipped her right back to the bed, until he was on top of her.

"Later," he whispered. "Much later. It'd be that long before the sight of you doesn't send me off the deep end."

And he centered himself at the heart of her and slowly entered, inch by inch.

She finally cried out, "Stop teasing me."

He plunged deep, until she was pinned in place, right beneath him.

"Dear God," she whispered. As he started to move, she realized nothing had prepared her for this. When she exploded in his arms, she laid weak and trembling beneath him, as he climaxed above her. When he finally crashed beside her and pulled her into his arms, she whispered, "You know that if I'd known this earlier …"

"It would always be like this," he said, trying to regain his breath. "I knew it. You knew it. You just needed to get there mentally."

She reached up and whispered, "Thank you for letting me get there in my own time."

"You're always welcome," he said, "but, if you think I'm letting you go anytime soon, you're wrong."

She smiled gently, rubbed her nose against him. "I hope not," she replied. "I don't want to get up anytime soon." As they lay here recuperating, she asked, "How do you think my cousin is?"

"I think he's just fine," Aiden stated. "He'll call me if he needs me."

"I thought it was supposed to be the other way around."

"It was before," he noted, "but now this is a whole new game. It's a whole new venture for the Mavericks. I don't know what will happen. All I can say is, right now, Mountain has a really big problem up there, and he has asked for help. And the Mavericks, being Mavericks, have answered the call."

"Just like you guys did for me, *huh*?"

He smiled broadly. "Believe me. I'm the happiest man alive that I came to your assistance. I wasn't at all sure about this assignment, when I was told what the job was. However, once I realized Mountain was involved, I knew it was important, and it sure was," he murmured. "Besides, sometimes things like this can change your life."

"Are you saying I've changed your life?" she asked in a teasing voice.

"Absolutely you have," he admitted, "and I couldn't be happier."

# EPILOGUE

LIEUTENANT COMMANDER MASON Callister walked into the private office and stood in front of retired Navy Commander Doran Magellan.

"Mason, good to see you."

Yet the dry tone of voice and the scowl pinching the silver-haired man all belied his words. Mason had known Doran for over a decade, and their friendship had only grown over time.

Mason waited, as he watched the other man try to work the new high-tech phone system on his desk. With his hand circling the air above the black box, he appeared to hit buttons randomly.

Mason held back his amusement but to no avail.

"Why can't a phone be a phone anymore?" the commander snapped, as his glare shifted from Mason to the box and back.

Asking the commander if he needed help wouldn't make the older man feel any better, but sitting here and watching as he indiscriminately punched buttons was a struggle. "Is Helen away?" Mason asked.

"Yes, damn it. She's at lunch, and I need her to be at lunch." The commander's piercing gaze pinned Mason in place. "No one is to know you're here."

Solemn, Mason nodded. "Understood."

"Doran? Is that you?" A crotchety voice slammed into the room through the phone's speakers. "Get away from that damn phone. You keep clicking buttons in my ear. Get Helen in there to do this."

"No, she can't be here for this."

Silence came first, then a huge groan. "Damn it. Then you should have connected me last, so I don't have to sit here and listen to you fumbling around."

"Go pour yourself a damn drink then," Doran barked. "I'm working on the others."

A snort was his only response.

Mason bit the inside of his lip, as he really tried to hold back his grin. The retired commander had been hell on wheels while on active duty, and, even now, the retired part of his life seemed to be more of a euphemism than anything.

"Damn things …"

Mason looked around the dark mahogany office and the walls filled with photos, awards, medals. A life of purpose, accomplishment. And all of that had only piqued his interest during the initial call he'd received, telling him to be here at this time.

"Ah, got it."

Mason's eyebrows barely twitched, as the commander gave him a feral grin. "I'd rather lead a warship into battle than deal with some of today's technology."

As he was one of only a few commanders who'd been in a position to do such a thing, it said much about his capabilities.

And much about current technology.

The retired commander leaned back in his massive chair and motioned to the cart beside Mason. "Pour three cups."

*Interesting.* Mason walked a couple steps across the rich

tapestry-style carpet and lifted the silver service to pour coffee into three very down-to-earth-looking mugs.

"Black for me."

Mason picked up two cups and walked one over to Doran.

"Thanks." He leaned forward and snapped into the phone, "Everyone here?"

Multiple voices responded.

*Curiouser and curiouser.* Mason recognized several of the voices. Other relics of an era gone by. Although not a one would like to hear that, and, in good faith, it wasn't fair. Mason had thought each of these men were retired, had relinquished power. Yet, as he studied Doran in front of him, Mason had to wonder if any of them actually had passed the baton or if they'd only slid into the shadows. Was this planned with the government's authority? Or were these retirees a shadow group to the government?

The tangible sense of power and control oozed from Doran's words, tone, stature—his very pores. This man might be heading into his sunset years—based on a simple calculation of chronological years spent on the planet—but he was a long way from being out of the action.

"Mason ..." Doran began.

"Sir?"

"We've got a problem."

Mason narrowed his gaze and waited.

Doran's glare was hard, steely hard, with an icy glint. "Do you know the Mavericks?"

Mason's eyebrows shot up. The black ops division was one of those well-kept secrets, so, therefore, everyone knew about it. He gave a decisive nod. "I do."

"And you're involved in the logistics behind the ICE

training program in the Arctic, are you not?"

"I am." Now where was the commander going with this?

"Do you know another SEAL by the name of Mountain Rode? He's been working for the black ops Mavericks." At his own words, the commander shook his head. "What the hell was his mother thinking when she gave him that moniker?"

"She wasn't thinking anything," said the man with a hard voice from behind Mason.

He stiffened slightly, then relaxed as he recognized that voice too.

"She died giving birth to me. And my full legal name is Mountain Bear Rode. It was my father's doing."

The commander glared at the new arrival. "Did I say you could come in?"

"Yes." Mountain's voice was firm, yet a definitive note of affection filled his tone.

That emotion told Mason so much.

The commander harrumphed, then cleared his throat. "Mason, we're picking up a significant amount of chatter over that ICE training. Most of it good. Some of it the usual caterwauling we've come to expect every time we participate in a joint training mission. This one is set to run for six months, then to reassess."

Mason already knew this. But he waited for the commander to get around to why Mason was here, and, more important, what any of this had to do with the mountain of a man who now towered beside him.

The commander shifted his gaze to Mountain, but he remained silent.

Mason noted Mountain was not only physically big but damn imposing and severely pissed, seemingly barely holding back the forces within. His body language seemed to yell, *And the world will fix this, or I'll find the reason why.*

For a moment Mason felt sorry for the world.

Finally a voice spoke through the phone. "Mason, this is Alpha here. I run the Mavericks. We've got a problem with that ICE training center. Mountain, tell him."

Mason shifted to include Mountain in his field of vision. Mason wished the other men on the conference call were in the room too. It was one thing to deal with men you knew and could take the measure of; it was another when they were silent shadows in the background.

"My brother is one of the men who reported for the Arctic training three weeks ago."

"Tergan Rode?" Mason confirmed. "I'm the one who arranged for him to go up there. He's a great kid."

A glimmer of a smile cracked Mountain's stony features. He nodded. "Indeed. A bright light in my often dark world. He's a dozen years younger than me, just passed his BUD/s training this spring, and raring to go. Until his raring to go then got up and went."

*Oh, shit.* Mason's gaze zinged to the commander, who had kicked up his feet to rest atop the big desk. Stocking feet. With Mickey Mouse images dancing on them. Sidetracked, Mason struggled to pull his attention back to Mountain. "Meaning?"

"He's disappeared." Mountain let out a harsh breath, as if just saying that out loud, and maybe to the right people, could allow him to relax—at least a little.

The commander spoke up. "We need your help, Mason. You're uniquely qualified for this problem."

It didn't sound as if he was qualified in any way for anything he'd heard so far. "Clarify." His spoken word was simplicity itself, but the tone behind it said he wanted the cards on the table … now.

Mountain spoke up. "He's the fifth incident."

Mason's gaze narrowed, as the reports from the training camp rolled through his mind. "Four dead. One was Russian. One was from the German SEAL team. Two were our men. All four were deemed accidental deaths."

"Except they weren't."

There it was. The root of the problem in black-and-white. He studied Mountain, aiming for neutrality. "Do you have evidence?"

"My brother did."

"Ah, hell."

Mountain gave a clipped nod. "I'm going to find him."

"Of that I have no doubt," Mason said quietly. "Do you have a copy of the evidence he collected?"

"I have some of it." Mountain held out a USB key. "This is your copy. Top secret."

"We don't have to remind you, Mason, that lives are at stake," Doran added. "Nor do we need another international incident. Consider also that a group of scientists, studying global warming, is close by, and not too far away is a village, home to a few hardy locals."

Mason accepted the key, turned to the commander, and asked, "Do we know whether this is internal or enemy warfare?"

"We don't know at this point," Alpha replied through the phone. "Mountain will lead Shadow Recon. His mission is twofold. One, find out what's behind these so-called accidents and put a stop to it by any means necessary. Two, locate his brother, hopefully alive."

"And where do I come in?" Mason asked.

"We want you to pull together a special team. The members of Shadow Recon will report to both you and Mountain, just in case."

That was clear enough.

"You'll stay stateside but in constant communication with Mountain—with the caveat that, if necessary, you're on the next flight out."

"What about bringing in other members from the Mavericks?" Mason suggested.

Alpha took this question too, his response coming through via Speakerphone. "We don't have the numbers. The budget for our division has been cut. So we called the commander to pull some strings."

That was Doran's cue to explain further. "Mountain has fought hard to get me on board with this plan, and I'm here now. The navy has a special budget for Shadow Recon and will take care of Mountain and you, Mason, and the team you provide."

"Skills needed?"

"Everything," Mountain said, his voice harsh. "But the highest priority is that these men need to operate in the shadows, mostly alone, without a team beside them. Too many new arrivals will alert the enemy. If we make any changes to the training program, it will raise alarms. We'll move the men in one or two at a time on the same rotation that the trainees are running right now."

"And when we get to the bottom of this?" Mason looked from the commander back to Mountain.

"Then the training can resume as usual," Doran stated.

Mason immediately churned through the names of possible team members, already popping up in his mind. How much could he tell his men? Obviously not much. Hell, he didn't know much himself. How much time did he have? "Timeline?"

The commander's final word told him of the urgency.

"Yesterday."


This concludes Book 18 of The Mavericks: Aiden.

Read about Magnus: Shadow Recon, Book 1

# Magnus: Shadow Recon
# (Book #1)

Deep in the permafrost of the Arctic, a joint task force, comprised of over one dozen countries, comes together to level up their winter skills. A mix of personalities, nationalities, and egos bring out the best—and the worst—as these globally elite men and women work and play together. They rub elbows with hardy locals and a group of scientists gathered close by …

One fatality is almost expected with this training. A second is tough but not a surprise. However, when a third goes missing? It's hard to not be suspicious. When the missing man is connected to one of the elite Maverick team members and is a special friend of Lieutenant Commander Mason Callister? All hell breaks loose …

Find book 1 here!

To find out more visit Dale Mayer's website.

https://geni.us/DMSRMagnusUniversal

# Chapter 1 of new
# SHADOW RECON Series

MOUNTAIN BEAR RODE landed on the vast wide polar expanse of the frozen north. A vehicle was supposed to be waiting for him, but one of the big Arctic Cats that operated up here was the best bet. As he exited the plane, he felt the chill already soaking through his parka. He shouldered his duffel bag and headed to the small shed that passed as a hangar. Inside was at least one of the two men Mason had waiting for him. Mason was hoping to stay stateside, and Mountain would do what he could. However, if he needed Mason, Mountain would call, and he knew Mason would come.

In the meantime perfectly capable men would help Mountain. Aiden was one of them, currently stateside too. Not that he had any plans to come to this frozen hellhole if he could help it either. But he was a Maverick and was promised to Mountain as part of his team for the duration of this job. And Mountain was damn glad to have Aiden. Mountain needed someone, multiple someones, on the outside to help sort out this mess and to gather intel, so no one inside would be suspicious. That would come. But Mountain needed to stave it off as long as possible.

He studied the tall bean pole in front of him. Mountain had done research on this man; so far, it all looked okay.

There were few enough men Mountain could say that about, and luckily Magnus was one of them. "Hey," Mountain greeted him, reaching out to shake his hand. However, the grim look on Magnus's face had Mountain asking, "What have you got?"

"Nothing good. No sign of your brother, and now another man is gone missing too. We've got a brand-new team flying in. Should arrive in a few minutes." He motioned at the hangar around him. "We're waiting for them to come in and to bring them back with us."

Mountain nodded.

Magnus didn't know the expected team was Mountain's; nobody was allowed to know. Not until they got to the bottom of whatever the hell was going on up here. Nobody could be suspicious.

"These missing men, … anything like that happen here before?"

"A certain number of deaths can always be expected in these severe-weather training missions." Magnus glared at the white snow-capped mountains around the small airport. "Nothing's harder than military training in extreme cold temperatures and with extreme exposure," he explained. "So believe me. Nobody is thinking these missing guys are anything out of the ordinary. They're just bodies we haven't found yet."

And that was just BS as far as Mountain was concerned. Men should be dying for their respective countries; they shouldn't be dying for the training, but Mountain would find out what was going on as soon as he got to the camp. "How many men are coming in?" he asked.

"Eight," Magnus replied.

At that, he stared at him. "I expected you to say six," he

replied, trying to cover his gaffe.

"Eight and two are women."

"*Hmm*," he said, frowning.

"Yeah, I don't know how the women will handle it," Magnus noted, "but you already know that you can't talk to the brass at all."

And that was the damn truth. The brass made decisions that often had nothing to do with reality. Mountain was here now; he'd find his damn brother even if it killed him. And it probably would.

Find book 1 here!

To find out more visit Dale Mayer's website.

https://geni.us/DMSRMagnusUniversal

# Author's Note

Thank you for reading Aiden: The Mavericks, Book 18! If you enjoyed the book, please take a moment and leave a short review.

Dear reader,

I love to hear from readers, and you can contact me at my website: www.dalemayer.com or at my Facebook author page. To be informed of new releases and special offers, sign up for my newsletter or follow me on BookBub. And if you are interested in joining Dale Mayer's Reader Group, here is the Facebook sign up page.
http://geni.us/DaleMayerFBGroup

Cheers,
Dale Mayer

# About the Author

Dale Mayer is a *USA Today* best-selling author, best known for her SEALs military romances, her Psychic Visions series, and her Lovely Lethal Garden cozy series. Her contemporary romances are raw and full of passion and emotion (Broken But … Mending, Hathaway House series). Her thrillers will keep you guessing (Kate Morgan, By Death series), and her romantic comedies will keep you giggling (*It's a Dog's Life*, a stand-alone novella; and the Broken Protocols series, starring Charming Marvin, the cat).

Dale honors the stories that come to her—and some of them are crazy, break all the rules and cross multiple genres!

To go with her fiction, she also writes nonfiction in many different fields, with books available on résumé writing, companion gardening, and the US mortgage system. All her books are available in print and ebook format.

## Connect with Dale Mayer Online

*Dale's Website – www.dalemayer.com*

*Twitter – @DaleMayer*

*Facebook Page – geni.us/DaleMayerFBFanPage*

*Facebook Group – geni.us/DaleMayerFBGroup*

*BookBub – geni.us/DaleMayerBookbub*

*Instagram – geni.us/DaleMayerInstagram*

*Goodreads – geni.us/DaleMayerGoodreads*

*Newsletter – geni.us/DaleNews*

# Also by Dale Mayer

## Published Adult Books:

**Shadow Recon**
Magnus, Book 1

**Bullard's Battle**
Ryland's Reach, Book 1
Cain's Cross, Book 2
Eton's Escape, Book 3
Garret's Gambit, Book 4
Kano's Keep, Book 5
Fallon's Flaw, Book 6
Quinn's Quest, Book 7
Bullard's Beauty, Book 8
Bullard's Best, Book 9
Bullard's Battle, Books 1–2
Bullard's Battle, Books 3–4
Bullard's Battle, Books 5–6
Bullard's Battle, Books 7–8

**Terkel's Team**
Damon's Deal, Book 1
Wade's War, Book 2
Gage's Goal, Book 3
Calum's Contact, Book 4
Rick's Road, Book 5
Scott's Summit, Book 6

Brody's Beast, Book 7

## Kate Morgan
Simon Says… Hide, Book 1
Simon Says… Jump, Book 2
Simon Says… Ride, Book 3
Simon Says… Scream, Book 4
Simon Says… Run, Book 5

## Hathaway House
Aaron, Book 1
Brock, Book 2
Cole, Book 3
Denton, Book 4
Elliot, Book 5
Finn, Book 6
Gregory, Book 7
Heath, Book 8
Iain, Book 9
Jaden, Book 10
Keith, Book 11
Lance, Book 12
Melissa, Book 13
Nash, Book 14
Owen, Book 15
Percy, Book 16
Quinton, Book 17
Ryatt, Book 18
Hathaway House, Books 1–3
Hathaway House, Books 4–6
Hathaway House, Books 7–9

**The K9 Files**

Ethan, Book 1
Pierce, Book 2
Zane, Book 3
Blaze, Book 4
Lucas, Book 5
Parker, Book 6
Carter, Book 7
Weston, Book 8
Greyson, Book 9
Rowan, Book 10
Caleb, Book 11
Kurt, Book 12
Tucker, Book 13
Harley, Book 14
Kyron, Book 15
Jenner, Book 16
Rhys, Book 17
The K9 Files, Books 1–2
The K9 Files, Books 3–4
The K9 Files, Books 5–6
The K9 Files, Books 7–8
The K9 Files, Books 9–10
The K9 Files, Books 11–12

**Lovely Lethal Gardens**

Arsenic in the Azaleas, Book 1
Bones in the Begonias, Book 2
Corpse in the Carnations, Book 3
Daggers in the Dahlias, Book 4
Evidence in the Echinacea, Book 5
Footprints in the Ferns, Book 6

Gun in the Gardenias, Book 7
Handcuffs in the Heather, Book 8
Ice Pick in the Ivy, Book 9
Jewels in the Juniper, Book 10
Killer in the Kiwis, Book 11
Lifeless in the Lilies, Book 12
Murder in the Marigolds, Book 13
Nabbed in the Nasturtiums, Book 14
Offed in the Orchids, Book 15
Poison in the Pansies, Book 16
Quarry in the Quince, Book 17
Revenge in the Roses, Book 18
Silenced in the Sunflowers, Book 19
Lovely Lethal Gardens, Books 1–2
Lovely Lethal Gardens, Books 3–4
Lovely Lethal Gardens, Books 5–6
Lovely Lethal Gardens, Books 7–8
Lovely Lethal Gardens, Books 9–10

## Psychic Vision Series

Tuesday's Child
Hide 'n Go Seek
Maddy's Floor
Garden of Sorrow
Knock Knock…
Rare Find
Eyes to the Soul
Now You See Her
Shattered
Into the Abyss
Seeds of Malice
Eye of the Falcon

Itsy-Bitsy Spider
Unmasked
Deep Beneath
From the Ashes
Stroke of Death
Ice Maiden
Snap, Crackle…
What If…
Talking Bones
String of Tears
Psychic Visions Books 1–3
Psychic Visions Books 4–6
Psychic Visions Books 7–9

## By Death Series
Touched by Death
Haunted by Death
Chilled by Death
By Death Books 1–3

## Broken Protocols – Romantic Comedy Series
Cat's Meow
Cat's Pajamas
Cat's Cradle
Cat's Claus
Broken Protocols 1-4

## Broken and… Mending
Skin
Scars
Scales (of Justice)
Broken but… Mending 1-3

## Glory

Genesis

Tori

Celeste

Glory Trilogy

## Biker Blues

Morgan: Biker Blues, Volume 1

Cash: Biker Blues, Volume 2

## SEALs of Honor

Mason: SEALs of Honor, Book 1

Hawk: SEALs of Honor, Book 2

Dane: SEALs of Honor, Book 3

Swede: SEALs of Honor, Book 4

Shadow: SEALs of Honor, Book 5

Cooper: SEALs of Honor, Book 6

Markus: SEALs of Honor, Book 7

Evan: SEALs of Honor, Book 8

Mason's Wish: SEALs of Honor, Book 9

Chase: SEALs of Honor, Book 10

Brett: SEALs of Honor, Book 11

Devlin: SEALs of Honor, Book 12

Easton: SEALs of Honor, Book 13

Ryder: SEALs of Honor, Book 14

Macklin: SEALs of Honor, Book 15

Corey: SEALs of Honor, Book 16

Warrick: SEALs of Honor, Book 17

Tanner: SEALs of Honor, Book 18

Jackson: SEALs of Honor, Book 19

Kanen: SEALs of Honor, Book 20

Nelson: SEALs of Honor, Book 21

Taylor: SEALs of Honor, Book 22

## Heroes for Hire

## SEALs of Steel

SEALs of Steel, Books 5–8
SEALs of Steel, Books 1–8

## The Mavericks
Kerrick, Book 1
Griffin, Book 2
Jax, Book 3
Beau, Book 4
Asher, Book 5
Ryker, Book 6
Miles, Book 7
Nico, Book 8
Keane, Book 9
Lennox, Book 10
Gavin, Book 11
Shane, Book 12
Diesel, Book 13
Jerricho, Book 14
Killian, Book 15
Hatch, Book 16
Corbin, Book 17
Aiden, Book 18
The Mavericks, Books 1–2
The Mavericks, Books 3–4
The Mavericks, Books 5–6
The Mavericks, Books 7–8
The Mavericks, Books 9–10
The Mavericks, Books 11–12

## Collections
Dare to Be You...
Dare to Love...
Dare to be Strong...

RomanceX3

## Standalone Novellas
It's a Dog's Life
Riana's Revenge
Second Chances

# Published Young Adult Books:

## Family Blood Ties Series
Vampire in Denial
Vampire in Distress
Vampire in Design
Vampire in Deceit
Vampire in Defiance
Vampire in Conflict
Vampire in Chaos
Vampire in Crisis
Vampire in Control
Vampire in Charge
Family Blood Ties Set 1–3
Family Blood Ties Set 1–5
Family Blood Ties Set 4–6
Family Blood Ties Set 7–9
Sian's Solution, A Family Blood Ties Series Prequel
    Novelette

## Design series
Dangerous Designs
Deadly Designs
Darkest Designs
Design Series Trilogy

**Standalone**

In Cassie's Corner

Gem Stone (a Gemma Stone Mystery)

Time Thieves

# Published Non-Fiction Books:

**Career Essentials**

Career Essentials: The Résumé

Career Essentials: The Cover Letter

Career Essentials: The Interview

Career Essentials: 3 in 1

www.ingramcontent.com/pod-product-compliance
Lightning Source LLC
Chambersburg PA
CBHW071434200726
48294CB00002B/626